The Revenge of Iron Eyes

When infamous bounty hunter Iron Eyes arrives in Silver Springs on the trail of two deadly outlaws he finds that they have already killed and maimed dozens of people inside the town's hotel before fleeing.

Although two other bounty hunters are after the same prey, Iron Eyes heads out into Apache country after the outlaws and the rest of their gang.

Unlike the other bounty hunters, this time Iron Eyes is not driven by the prices on the outlaws' heads. This time it's different. This time it's personal: the Revenge of Iron Eyes.

The Revenge of Iron Eyes

Rory Black

A Black Horse Western

ROBERT HALE · LONDON

ISBN 978-0-7090-8608-6

Robert Hale Limited
Clerkenwell House
Clerkenwell Green
London EC1R 0HT

www.halebooks.com

Typeset by
Derek Doyle & Associates, Shaw Heath
Printed and bound in Great Britain by
CPI Antony Rowe, Wiltshire

Dedicated to Tony and Julia Phillips with gratitude.

PROLOGUE

Blood no longer ran down the walls as it had done an hour earlier. Now it simply clung and congealed to the very fabric of the hotel's interior. Flies were already gathering as the mid-afternoon heat started to fill the building with the acrid aroma of death. The townsfolk had rescued the wounded and carried them to the doctor's office at the end of the sunbaked street, yet they seemed unwilling or perhaps just afraid to venture close to those who had been slain.

The bodies were scattered throughout the large foyer of the hotel. A trail of gore and entrails, like gruesome cobwebs, criss-crossed the blood-soaked carpeted floor.

As the smell grew even more sickening the lone horseman headed into the outskirts of Silver Springs. Every eye was upon him. They watched the strange unholy figure as he jabbed his large, sharp spurs into the flesh of his tired mount to encourage it on after the tracks he was following.

As the gentle desert breeze blew his mane of matted hair off his shoulders a gasp from the crowd filled the street. None of them had ever seen a sight so horrific.

His long legs hung to either side of his exhausted pony as he slid his boots from the stirrups. The infamous bounty hunter, Iron Eyes, had trailed his two quarries to this remote town with the knowledge that both outlaws could be legally killed for the reward money on their heads.

The skeletal fingers eased back on the reins. He stopped the mount at the hitching rail just outside the hotel and watched as the crowd of curious onlookers parted until he could see the open doorway.

A man with a star pinned to a black vest pushed his way through the crowd until he was standing on the edge of the boardwalk. The man could not conceal his shock when he focused on the face of the bounty hunter.

'Who are you?' he managed to ask.

Iron Eyes threw his right leg over the neck of the pony and slid to the dry ground. A small plume of dust rose and encircled him.

'They call me Iron Eyes!' he stated.

The sheriff watched as the thin figure mounted the steps until he was standing on the boardwalk. He felt his knees start to knock as he realized that this man looked even worse the closer he got.

'You know anything about this?' the sheriff used his thumb to point back at the open doorway behind him.

Iron Eyes sniffed the air. He could smell death in both his flared nostrils. 'There bin some killing here!'

'I asked you a question, mister!' the lawman repeated. 'Do you know anything about this? You a member of the gang who done this?'

'I ain't vermin!' There was a look of disgust on the face of the bounty hunter as he placed a hand on the shoulder of the sheriff and pushed him aside. 'I kill vermin! Kill 'em dead!'

'Don't you go laying hands on me!' The sheriff made as though to grab the closer arm of Iron Eyes, then he felt the cold steel of the gun barrel push under his throat.

'Ease down, Sheriff!' Iron Eyes whispered. 'I'm a bounty hunter! I reckon the two boys I'm hunting done this! Their horse tracks lead right up to the hitching pole!'

The sheriff took a step back and swallowed hard. He watched as the Navy Colt was returned to the thin man's belt next to its twin.

'Who are they?'

Iron Eyes paused by the door, allowing his narrowed eyes to adjust to the darker interior of the hotel.

'One is called Duke Layne and the other is Matt

Craven!' he informed the sheriff. 'Two real bad killers by all accounts!'

The sheriff stood beside the taller man and waved his arms around. 'Why would they do this?'

Iron Eyes took a deep breath. 'This is what they do, Sheriff! This is why they're wanted dead or alive across three states and territories! They kill cos they like it! Ain't no reason for some critters' actions! Like I said, they're just vermin! Two-legged vermin!'

'We ain't never had no trouble here before!' the lawman said with a shrug. 'Nothing like this, anyways!'

Iron Eyes nodded. 'Was there money in the safe?'

'Reckon so! We had us a few wealthy folks visiting from back East! They must have had themselves a pretty penny by the way they was heeled!'

'Craven and Layne tend to go looking for rich folks and hotels are easier than banks to hold up!' Iron Eyes handed two crumpled Wanted posters from one of his pockets to the sheriff. 'Makes mighty interesting reading!'

'But why kill so many?' The sheriff gulped.

'They must have gotten themselves cornered, I guess.' Iron Eyes walked in to the foyer. 'Or maybe they just liked the idea of killing defenceless folks!'

The sheriff was about to follow but stopped when he saw the bounty hunter glance at him. It was the ice-cold look of a man who did not want to be trailed. When the lawman stared down at the once pristine carpet, he decided that he would allow Iron Eyes to investigate on his own.

The spurs rang out and echoed off the walls as Iron Eyes carefully picked his way between the bodies, which seemed to stretch out in every direction. Expensive leather furniture had also taken a lot of lead and horsehair stuffing was everywhere. When he reached the other end of the large room, Iron Eyes stopped and stared at the carnage which surrounded him.

So many bodies, he thought.

There were bodies everywhere. Men, women and children had all fallen victim to the outlaws' deadly lead.

'This is bad,' the sheriff called across the foyer. 'Darn bad!'

Iron Eyes pushed a cigar between his teeth and chewed it as his fingers found a match in his shirt pocket. His thumbnail ran across its tip. He raised his hand and sucked in the flame. Smoke drifted from his mouth.

'Yep!' the bounty hunter agreed. He inhaled deeply and walked back towards the sheriff. 'Any idea which way they headed?'

'You still after them? After ya seen this you're still gonna take them on?'

'They're worth a lotta gold, old-timer!' Iron Eyes

11

said as he reached the boardwalk. 'And I'm kinda shy of gold right now!'

The sheriff's expression altered. 'I thought maybe the sight of all them bodies might have been the spur to make you go after them two bastards, boy! Not gold!'

Iron Eyes raised a twisted eyebrow. 'I've seen a lot of dead folks in my time, Sheriff. Too many to get upset by it!'

'There's young kids strewn out on that floor!' the sheriff raised his voice in disbelief. 'Surely you feel something, don't you?'

Iron Eyes brooded for a moment. Eventually he nodded. 'Yeah, I do feel something now you mention it!'

'What do you feel, Iron Eyes?'

'Thirsty!' Iron Eyes said through the corner of his mouth. 'Go get me a couple of bottles of whiskey!'

'You ain't human!' the lawman protested.

Iron Eyes shrugged and pushed the long hair off his scarred face with his bony fingers.

'I'm the one who'll be headed out after them, ain't I? I'm the one who'll be facing their lead, not you! Go get me that whiskey and you can stay here with the rest of these spineless critters, nice and safe!'

The sheriff knew that the tall bounty hunter was right. He would be the one who would lay his life on the line, not any of the menfolk of Silver Springs who watched, open-mouthed. He stepped down into the sun and headed towards the closest saloon.

Iron Eyes unscrewed the stoppers of his canteens, dropped them both into the water trough and watched the bubbles as they slowly filled.

Suddenly he heard a faint sound behind him. It was coming from the hotel. Iron Eyes dropped the canteens into the water and turned. He listened hard. The sound of a child whimpering came to his ears. Without a moment's hesitation he strode back into the stinking hotel lobby and paused for a brief moment until his honed senses located the child. His eyes narrowed. He stared at the crumpled mound of bodies to his left and then saw a small hand move from behind the blood-soaked body of a woman.

Iron Eyes spat the cigar at the floor and strode to the child. His thin cheeks sucked in at the sight. He knelt in the blood and plucked the small girl up as if she weighed little more than a feather. Within seconds he was back out on the street with the child cradled in his arms.

A gasp went around the people who did nothing but watch.

'Where's the doc?' He yelled at the top of his voice. 'This kid's dying! Where's the doc?'

13

Some hands pointed down the street. His eyes narrowed and focused on a weathered shingle which hung from a porch some way along. Without knowing why, Iron Eyes ran towards his goal. With each long stride he felt the child's blood dripping through her clothing over his bare hands.

Sheriff Chet Bodine had just stepped out from the saloon with the two whiskey bottles in his hands when he saw the bounty hunter running with the wounded child in his arms towards Doc Jackson's office. A knowing look etched his face.

'Like it or not, you are human, Iron Eyes!' he muttered to himself.

Like a mother hen watching over her brood, Iron Eyes remained in the corner of the doctor's office, observing the medical man's every move as he carefully removed the last of the three bullets which had hit the small girl back at the hotel. The sound of the lead ball as it dropped into the white enamel tray echoed around the lantern-lit surgery.

Doc Jackson glanced at the tall silent figure. 'Can you help me here, son?'

Iron Eyes was startled by the question. 'You want me to help you? How?'

'I gotta stitch this young 'un up!' Jackson explained. 'I want you to help mop up the blood while I sew her up!'

The bounty hunter walked to the table. He picked up the clean rags and wiped the blood from the girl's pale white skin as the doctor feverishly worked.

'Will she be OK?' Iron Eyes asked.

'Hard to tell, son!' Jackson replied. 'It'll go one way or the other by dawn!'

Iron Eyes nodded. 'Reckon I'll hang around here and see how it goes, Doc!'

'I thought you had other business!' Jackson said. 'The sheriff said you were a bounty hunter on the trail of the bastards who did this! How come you ain't lit out after them already?'

'There ain't no rush!' Iron Eyes dipped the rag into a bowl of warm water and then ran the cloth across the girl's face. 'I'll catch up with them soon enough! When I do they're dead!'

Jackson sighed. 'Her name's Holly Barker!'

Iron Eyes stared down at the helpless girl. He nodded.

ONE

The night had fallen quickly and a chill had replaced the blistering heat of the day. Yet Iron Eyes had not noticed. To him all there was to life was the vengeance he dished out to all those who were wanted, dead or alive. He descended the wooden steps from the second-storey offices of Abraham Jackson, MD, and paused beneath the flickering street-light. He fumbled for a fresh cigar in his deep pockets but found only bullets for his pair of deadly Navy Colts.

'About time you come down from there, son!' Sheriff Bodine said from the shadows where he sat on one of the two hard chairs that were propped up against the store front.

The bounty hunter was like a mountain cat. Even during the darkest of nights his eyes could see things most normal men could never have observed.

16

'You got a smoke there, old-timer?'

'Reckon I could stretch to lending you a cigar!' Bodine said.

Iron Eyes walked to the vacant chair and sat. He accepted the long, thin cigar and pushed it between his teeth.

'Much obliged!'

The lawman struck a match and offered its flame to the bounty hunter. 'How is she?'

Iron Eyes sucked in the smoke and let it dwell inside his lungs for a moment before exhaling. 'The doc won't know for sure until after sun-up!'

Bodine pulled his pocket watch from his vest pocket and opened its silver case. He held his arm out until the lantern-light illuminated its face. He snapped it shut and rose to his feet.

'The ten o'clock stage will be in soon!' he said.

Iron Eyes stood. 'What time is it?' he asked.

'Nearly midnight!'

'That's why I ain't got a watch!' Iron Eyes followed the sheriff across the street towards the Overland Stage depot. 'You expecting someone?'

'Yep!' Bodine answered. 'Andrew Barker!'

'Is he kin of the little girl?'

'Her father!'

Just as they stepped up on to the boardwalk the telegraph worker rushed from his office and waved at them. He was a small, balding man as thin as any man could get without being dead.

17

'Sheriff Bodine!'

Both men paused and waited until the small thin man reached them. He was puffing hard and had to rest a hand upon a wooden upright before he could speak again.

'The telegraph is down west of here—' he gasped.

'How'd you know?' Iron Eyes interrupted.

'I've bin trying to wire Drover's Gulch but the wires must be down!'

'But it was OK when you wired Andrew Barker in Durango for me earlier!' Bodine said.

'Durango is north of here, Sheriff!' the thin man panted. 'Them's different wires! They're all OK exceptin' for the one west!'

Iron Eyes inhaled deeply and savoured the smoke. 'That means the vermin I'm hunting went west! They must have shot the wires off their poles! What was the name of the town you spoke of?'

'Drover's Gulch! Why?'

'Cos that's where I'm headed!' Iron Eyes spat.

A dozen yards down the boardwalk the swing doors of the Red Pepper saloon pushed open and a burly man stepped out into the night air. Smoke from a half-chewed cigarette twisted around his battered Stetson. He glared up at the three contrasting figures near the stage depot and growled.

'I thought it was you, Iron Eyes!'

18

Bodine scratched his whiskered chin and looked up at the steel-cold face of the bounty hunter.

'You know that critter?'

'Yep!' Iron Eyes replied. 'I know him OK! That's Buffalo Benson from Utah! He's a bounty hunter of sorts, like me!'

The thin man rushed back to the safety of the telegraph office, hastily bolted its door and pulled down the blinds.

The burly figure squared up to Iron Eyes and rested his huge hands on his holstered gun grips. There was an arrogance about him which defied logic.

'I hear that you're on the trail of two outlaws with my name on their hides!' Benson gruffed. 'Reckon ya better find yourself some other prey this time! That bounty belongs to me!'

Iron Eyes began to reduce the distance between them with long contemptuous strides.

'When did you ride in, Buffalo?'

'A couple of hours back!' Benson answered. 'You was busy up in the doc's playing nursemaid!'

'I ain't no nursemaid!' Iron Eyes kept walking towards Benson. He gripped the cigar firmly between his teeth and stared hard at the man before him.

'I'd heard tell that ya bin getting soft!' Benson laughed deeply.

Iron Eyes stopped. There were only four feet

19

separating the two bounty hunters. Although Iron Eyes was far taller, he knew that Benson was probably twice his weight.

'I ain't giving you my bounty, Buffalo!' he snarled.

'Then I'd better make sure I takes it!' Benson glared.

For what seemed like an eternity neither man moved a muscle. Only tobacco smoke moved around their statuesque forms. Bodine was about to approach them when he saw the heavier man drag both his guns from their holsters. The sheriff froze to the spot and watched in awe as Iron Eyes' long arms reached the weapons and prevented them from being raised. Then Iron Eyes' long, thin left leg kicked up and the mule-ear boot caught Benson in his crotch.

A sickening gasp bellowed out of the heavier bounty hunter. He dropped both guns and buckled. Iron Eyes pulled one of his own guns and cracked its blue steel barrel across the top of Benson's hat. The man fell in a heap.

'I . . . I thought you were gonna shoot him for a second, son!' Bodine said.

Iron Eyes pushed his gun back into his belt and turned. He pointed at the stage which had just entered the wide street and was heading to the depot.

'There's the stage, Sheriff!' he said.

'Why didn't you shoot him?' Bodine asked. 'It would have been self-defence cos he was gonna shoot you!'

'Ain't no price on Buffalo's head!' Iron Eyes replied. 'I don't waste bullets on worthless folks! I'd be obliged if'n you'd lock him up for a few days, though!'

'For attempted murder?'

Iron Eyes headed towards the livery where his horse had been taken earlier that day.

'Nah, make it for just being ugly!'

Somewhere ten miles outside the town of Silver Springs the outlaws had separated. Iron Eyes held his reins to his chest and stared at both sets of hoof tracks. One set went north up through dense brush whilst the other led straight on. Whatever lay in that direction, it was as yet unknown to the bounty hunter. But Iron Eyes knew that it had to lead to Drover's Gulch because the long line of telegraph poles stretched out for as far as the eye could see.

Iron Eyes dragged the neck of his pony hard and drove the animal up north into the brush. He knew that there were several small settlements along this route and judging by the length of both sets of tracks, this outlaw was not pushing his mount as hard as his companion.

This horseman might be easier to catch up with,

Iron Eyes told himself as he thundered through the avenue of trees set below smooth-faced over-hanging rocks.

A string of remote ranch houses marked the long dusty trail and the bounty hunter started to recognize the area. He had been here before on the heels of other fleeing outlaws.

Then, as he forced the pony over a high rise, he spotted the chestnut mare which he knew belonged to Duke Layne tied to a rough wooden fence line outside a ramshackle building set fifty or more feet off the trail.

Iron Eyes slowed his mount and then steered it between a group of trees. He dismounted swiftly and tied his reins to a stout branch.

Smoke traced its way up into the blue afternoon sky from a stone chimney set at the side of the small house. Iron Eyes wondered who, if anyone, lived in this place where Layne had stopped. Then another question filtered into his mind.

Why had Layne stopped here? It kept gnawing at the bounty hunter as he made his way through the brush. The house appeared deserted. There was no livestock anywhere around the place.

Most of the other ranch houses he had ridden past had flocks of chickens surrounding the main buildings. This place appeared devoid of all stock.

When Iron Eyes reached the boundary fence he stopped and stared across the distance between himself and the weathered building. Its windows had broken glass planes in rotting frames.

He stepped between the poles and straightened up. His hands drew the matched Navy Colts from his belt. He cocked both hammers and continued to move like a panther towards the side of the building.

With every step his keen eyes searched the wooden structure for signs of movement. For just the merest hint of life. A life he was determined to end.

Then just before he reached the side wall, a noise to his left drew him around on his high heels. He went to shoot when he saw the face looking at him with large blue eyes.

It was a female. No more than twelve or thirteen years of age. She wore blue overalls and a ragged shirt tucked into them.

Somehow, the bounty hunter managed to curb his deadly instincts. He almost fell to his knees with the sheer effort of not squeezing the triggers of his weapons.

'W-who are you?' her shaking voice asked.

Iron Eyes glared in total disbelief. This was not the ruthless outlaw he sought. This was nothing like Duke Layne, his mind screamed at him.

'That horse!' he pointed with the barrel of his left Colt. 'Where's the man who belongs to that horse?'

'Gone!' she said bluntly.

'Gone?' Iron Eyes repeated the word. It was like a nail being driven into him.

'Yeah, long gone!' the girl added.

'That don't make no sense!' Iron Eyes moved toward her. She backed off an equal distance. They were no closer. 'I've bin chasing a killer named Duke Layne! Why would he leave his horse here?'

'He took my pa's grey!' she spat. 'He said his horse was spent. Worn out! He needed a fresh nag to take him someplace!'

Iron Eyes tucked one of his guns into his pants belt and rested a hand on the house wall.

'Which way did he head?'

'Wouldn't you like to know?' The girl laughed, curled one of her pigtails around her index finger, turned and walked away. Iron Eyes rubbed the sweat from his face, exhaled and shook his head. He strode quickly back to his pony. He knew that the outlaw had used his head. Both their horses were spent but now it was Layne who had a fresh mount under his saddle. Iron Eyes untied his reins and looked at his worn-out mount. Reluctantly, he decided to water the creature.

Iron Eyes lifted one of his canteens from the saddle horn and unscrewed its stopper.

Out of the corner of his eye he could see the young girl watching him from the corner of the shack. His thoughts drifted back to the wounded girl at Silver Springs. She had still been clinging to life when he had set out after the two outlaws. He wondered if she was still winning her battle.

When the Indian pony had drunk its fill the bounty hunter hauled his lean frame up on to the saddle and turned full circle. He started to retrace his own trail back to where the outlaws had parted company.

Now he would follow Craven.

TWO

The sheriff had been sitting on his chair for hours watching the unconscious Buffalo Benson lying stretched across the creaking cot behind the bars of the building's solitary cell. He lifted the black coffee pot and realized it was empty. Bodine rose to his feet, glanced out of the window at the dark street and then walked to the stove. He opened its small cast-iron door and tossed a few logs on to the flames. Sparks rose and were sucked up its chimney.

'Hey! You got any grub in this place?' Benson asked in a chilling voice.

The sheriff was startled. He turned his head and stared across at the man who had forced his bulky frame up into a sitting position before nursing his aching head.

'I can get ya some vittles!' Bodine said.

'Good!' the bounty hunter snarled. 'Go get it then!'

The lawman filled the coffee pot with water and ground coffee and placed it atop the stove. He closed the blackened door of the stove and then stared at the man. He was thankful that he had locked him up.

'In my own good time, Benson!'

Benson looked up at the sheriff. If looks could kill, Chet Bodine would have been already dead.

'How come I'm locked up in here? How come Iron Eyes ain't in here with me? You kin to that scarecrow? Let me out!'

'You don't frighten me, Benson!' the sheriff told him. 'I'm too damn old to be scared by trash like you! You're gonna stay there until the circuit judge hits town!'

Buffalo Benson stood up. He gave a long snort through his flared nostrils and then approached the bars. His huge hands gripped them and tested their strength.

'I've killed men for talking to me like that!'

'I still ain't feared of you!'

'You oughta be, old-timer!' Benson gave a slight smile. His eyes were fixed upon the window behind the desk.

'How come?' Sheriff Bodine sat down.

'Cos I didn't come to this damn town on my lonesome!' Benson released the grip of his left hand on the iron bar and pointed at the window behind the lawman's head. 'Look!'

The sheriff heard the sound of metal tapping on glass behind him and turned. A bullet shattered the glass pane and buried itself deep into his chest. Instinctively Bodine went to reach for his gun but then recalled that he had hung his belt on the hatstand beside the door. Before he could rise from his chair the door opened and a man entered quickly. Smoke still trailed from the barrel of his Smith & Wesson.

'About time you got here, Snake!' Benson snapped.

The man called Snake pounced on the sheriff, smashed the heel of his weapon across Bodine's head, plucked up the key ring and tossed it to his pard.

'I was waiting for you to wake up!' Snake said through yellowed teeth as Benson unlocked the cell door and grabbed his weapons off a table close to the stove. 'I sure weren't gonna carry ya to the horses!'

'Is that lawman dead, Snake?'

'He will be soon enough!'

'Good! C'mon!' the burly man ordered. 'We gotta catch up with Layne and Craven before Iron Eyes gets his claws into their bounty!'

'Iron Eyes?' Snake repeated the name as both men left the building and moved down the boardwalk to their horses.

Benson mounted. 'You sound scared, Snake!'

Snake Peters did not reply.

Drover's Gulch was a town on the very edge of civilization. None of the people who lived within the boundaries of the sprawling town knew anything about the niceties of such things. They considered themselves lucky to be alive and knew that death was their only certainty. These were not people who planned too far ahead. With the law so far away and most of the townspeople either belonging to or having connections with the numerous gangs who plied their deadly trade along the Texas–Mexican border, life tended to be short.

An acrid aroma filled the air and hung over the town. It was the stench of untold numbers of outhouses. Little lime was wasted here. Narrow lanes stank with the putrid excretions of those who relieved themselves wherever they wanted rather than find the designated outhouses.

Smoke drifted from the oil lanterns atop the poles that were dotted along the wide dusty streets. A strange orange-coloured glow flowed out at intervals. More light cascaded from the saloons which seemed to make up a fifth of the town's buildings.

The aroma of stale sawdust was mixed with the

sound of dozens of tinny pianos. It was as if the drinking-holes were in competition with one another, trying to lure men through their swing doors with the promise of cheap liquor and even cheaper female company. It did not take much to persuade customers anyway for most knew that they had better enjoy themselves now, for there might never be another opportunity.

By the standards of most border towns, Drover's Gulch appeared to be pretty well stocked with men and livestock. Horses were tied to hitching rails everywhere, but mostly outside the saloons and the buildings which displayed red lanterns in their windows.

Yet none of this meant a thing to the rider who aimed his forlorn Indian pony into the aromatic settlement. This was merely another place where the tracks of an outlaw had led him.

Iron Eyes was probably more notorious than any of those he tracked down and killed. No other bounty hunter could fill men with prices on their heads with more fear or dread.

For Iron Eyes only hunted one way. He chose only those wanted either dead or alive. That meant he could kill them and still claim the bounty.

There was no other way for the tall, emaciated rider. He had learned his hunting skills as a child left to fend for himself in the forests far to the east. To him, there was only one thing to do with anything you tracked and hunted. You killed it. When it had been animals he had trailed, he did it for their pelts and ate what was left.

When he had discovered that men could bring far greater profit, Iron Eyes had simply transferred his cold-blooded skills to critters with two legs.

There was nothing personal in his dispatching any of the men. They were just faces on Wanted posters. Faces with price tags printed in bold black ink. Men who, he knew, were beyond salvation. If the law said they could be killed, he just did it.

Iron Eyes sat astride the slow-walking pony. His long limp hair hung over his wide thin shoulders as he watched every one of the men who filled the boardwalks and streets. He steered the animal beneath him with one hand whilst the other gripped the handle of one of the matched Navy Colts that jutted from his belt.

Nothing was missed by the small burning eyes as they darted all around him from face to face. He knew that almost every face belonged to someone with a price on his head, but that did not matter to him. He was after one man and, like a hound with the scent of a fox in its nostrils, he would not be swayed until he found him. He did not seem to move a muscle. He just sat on the saddle and willed the thin pony on.

31

Another hideous scent filled the air. It was the smell of fear. Fear bred hatred. And everyone hated the very name of the strange killing rider. Even the Apache feared and hated Iron Eyes, for they knew he had no liking for them either. But the bounty hunter had never started a fight with any of the Indians he had met over the years.

There was no profit in killing men with no bounty on their heads. But he had killed them anyway when they had attacked him, and they always attacked him.

To the Apache, Iron Eyes was everything they hated in the white man, and more. To them he was the spirit of death. A lone rider who appeared to be invincible.

It was they who had started the myth that Iron Eyes was a ghost. Something it was impossible to kill.

Yet they always tried.

To the white men who had faced the awesome gunman, Iron Eyes appeared more like an Indian than a white man. His long black mane of hair and his weathered complexion seemed to confirm their theories, yet even Iron Eyes did not know the truth.

This was his fate. He was neither one thing nor the other. He had learned long ago that he would never be accepted by any race of two-legged critters.

32

He would remain alone!

His face bore witness to every fight and battle he had been involved in. Untended wounds and scars had twisted his features until they appeared more and more monstrous. He still carried lead from bullets which had never been cut from his thin, pitiful frame.

Maybe there was some truth in the stories of the bounty hunter who should have died years earlier. Maybe Iron Eyes *was* a ghost.

But could a ghost have drawn and fired his Navy Colts with such deadly accuracy?

Iron Eyes tapped his sharp spurs into the flesh of the pony and it increased its speed. The animal cantered up to the front of one of the saloons, where it was reined in hard. Every sinew in Iron Eyes' body told him that his prey was close. He sensed it.

In one fluid movement, the tall horseman swung his right leg over the head of the pony and slid from his saddle. Iron Eyes looped his reins over the end of the hitching pole and tied a secure knot.

He paused and stared at a bay mare whose reins were wrapped around a wooden upright. The horse was lathered up even more than his own pony. The bounty hunter strode to its side and the horse shied away. All horses sensed that this was one man who cared little for any living creatures.

Iron Eyes stared at the horse even harder.

This was the animal he had been tracking, he thought. This was the mount of the outlaw Matt Craven. And Craven was worth $1,000 dead or alive.

'What you looking at, stranger?' a voice asked from behind him.

Iron Eyes turned his head. His eyes burned into the questioner like branding-irons.

'Craven!' he muttered in a low whisper.

The man felt himself start to shake. It was as though the very sight of the hideous face had melted every scrap of his manhood.

He nodded and then rushed away.

Iron Eyes narrowed his eyes and looked up at the name painted on the wooden façade above the boardwalk.

'Five Aces Saloon!' he read aloud.

He stepped up and stared over the swing doors into the busy interior of the saloon. There were at least a hundred souls inside and they were all drunk.

He looked at the staircase to the right of the bar. Its carpet was threadbare from the patrons who continuously walked up and down with the barely dressed females. Boots and spurs had taken their toll. Iron Eyes could see four doors up on the landing but knew that there had to be more further back.

Craven could be up there, Iron Eyes thought.

He returned his attention to the people who filled the bar-room. So many of them that it was hard to tell where one figure started and another stopped. The bar was crowded and so was every table. The gaps between the tables were also filled. Men staggered in various stages of drunkenness as females encouraged them to drink until they would have the courage to take them up to one of the rooms above them.

The memory of the small child who had been caught in the murderous crossfire back at Silver Springs filled Iron Eyes again. Her dried blood still covered his sleeves and shirt front. If Craven was here he would certainly die, the bounty hunter silently vowed.

A man moved beside him and rested a hand on the top of the swing doors. Iron Eyes glanced at the man who was also looking into the saloon with interest.

'You looking for someone, mister?' the man asked without looking at Iron Eyes.

'Yep!'

'You a lawman?' the man drawled.

'Nope!' Iron Eyes replied. 'I'm a bounty hunter.'

'Figured as much!'

'What's it to you?'

'Nothing, except I reckon you don't know that

35

there ain't no law in Drover's Gulch.' the man sighed. 'You wanna kill someone here, you ain't gonna collect no bounty!'

Iron Eyes pulled a cigar from the deep pocket of his coat and placed it between his teeth. He pondered the information as his thin fingers located a match and struck it. He sucked in the smoke and then tossed the match over his shoulder.

'No law?' the bounty hunter repeated the statement through a cloud of grey smoke. 'None at all?'

'Used to be but this town kinda draws vermin and them rats killed old Sheriff Boone.' The man paused. 'Must be ten years back now. I was his deputy. I retired damn quick after that!'

Iron Eyes nodded.

'That makes it tough.' Iron Eyes inhaled and then allowed the smoke to drift down through his nostrils.

'Gotta be at least a hundred outlaws in this cesspit!' the man added. 'You kill one of them in Drover's Gulch and you got ninety-nine men shooting at you, son! Bad odds!'

'Damn bad odds!' Iron Eyes growled like a hound that had just seen its bone dragged from it. 'Reckon I'll have to kill the critter outside town!'

'It's a long ways to the nearest civilized town!' The man sighed again. 'The desert sun can rot a full-grown steer in less than a couple of days! You gotta kill him close to a town where there's some law in!'

Iron Eyes half-closed his eyes and looked hard at the man.

'How come you're so helpful?' he asked.

The man looked at Iron Eyes. He did not flinch. 'I told you that I used to be a deputy, boy. I was good but the way they killed the sheriff painted me yella! I'm still one of the good guys though!'

'What's your name?'

'Dooley! Buck Dooley!' the man replied. 'And you gotta be Iron Eyes!'

'How'd you know that?'

'I heard about you a long time ago!' Dooley looked back over the swing doors into the Five Aces. 'Mostly I heard what you looks like! Reckon there can't be another bounty hunter with your description, huh?'

'Damn right!' Iron Eyes pushed the doors open and walked into the saloon. 'C'mon, Dooley. I'm buying!'

Buck Dooley trailed the tall thin figure towards the bar. It was like the old Bible story. People parted before Iron Eyes just as the Red Sea had done when faced by Moses.

The Five Aces boasted two bartenders after sundown. They both saw the ominous figure of Iron Eyes as he strode across the sawdust-covered floor towards them. Neither man had ever seen anyone who looked quite like the bounty hunter.

Iron Eyes placed a boot on the brass rail and looked at the array of whiskey bottles stacked on shelves behind the two nervous bartenders. Dooley stood beside him and was amused to see the faces of the men across the bar counter.

'W-what'll it be?' the closer bartender asked.

'Whiskey!' Iron Eyes replied. 'Bottle!'

'And two glasses!' Dooley added.

One bartender plucked the bottle off the shelf as the other picked up the glasses. Iron Eyes watched silently as they were placed on the wet surface of the counter.

Suddenly a drunk pushed his way through the crowd towards the bar. He pulled Iron Eyes' arm.

'We don't want no redskins in the Five Aces!' he slurred noisily.

Iron Eyes stared at the red-faced man. 'You calling me an Indian?'

'I sure am! What else would you be with hair like this?' The man went to touch the long black hair.

It was a mistake.

Iron Eyes drew one of his Navy Colts, aimed at the floor and squeezed its trigger. The bullet hit the left boot of the drunk and blasted it apart. Then Iron Eyes used the gun grip to hit the man's chin. The drunk flew backwards and disappeared into the ocean of stunned faces.

Iron Eyes glanced around the room. The look in

his eyes was a silent warning to all of the onlookers that they would get the same if any of them dared to draw on him.

'Anyone else calls me an Injun will get the same or maybe worse!' he warned.

THREE

An hour or more earlier Andrew Barker had heard the gunshot through the open window of Doc Jackson's office, where he had been seated next to his seriously ill child. The slumbering physician had awoken and stood up instinctively. He rubbed his eyes, and then looked across at the anxious father, who was holding the unconscious Holly's hand.

'Did you hear that, Mr Barker?' Jackson asked. He moved to the bed and placed the back of his hand against the girl's temple. 'Was that a shot or was I dreaming?'

'You're right, Doc! I heard a shot as well!' Barker replied. 'I think it came from down the street somewhere!'

Jackson felt the small child's pulse and then rubbed his neck and sighed. He could not conceal

40

his anxiety about the girl's condition.

'Damn it all! How many more bullets are folks gonna waste around here? For years Silver Springs has been one of the quietest towns along the border and in a couple of days guns are going off all over the place!'

'I hear folks, Doc!' Barker said, staring at the window as its lace drapes fluttered in the evening breeze. 'A lotta folks by the sound of it! They're getting louder!'

'Sounds like they're headed here!' Jackson walked around the cot and raised the tobacco-stained lace. He stared down into the lantern-lit street and shook his head. 'Reckon that old saying must be right! There ain't no peace for the wicked!'

Barker came and stood beside him. 'You sure that they're headed here, Doc?'

'Yep! It's always the same! You hear a shot and then a crowd and then they bring up some idiot with a hole in him and I'm expected to save his life! I'm meant to produce a miracle! Mind you, if they don't come here then ya know the varmint is dead and he's being hauled off to the undertaker!'

Barker rested a hand on the doctor's shoulder. 'You produced a miracle for my little Holly, Doc! I'll be eternally grateful for that! Since her mother passed away she's all I have left!'

Jackson shrugged. 'She ain't out of the woods

41

yet, son! I thought she'd have woken up by now! I just can't figure it!'

'The man who brought her here!' Barker spoke in a hushed tone. 'What was his name?'

'Iron Eyes!' Jackson felt a chill trace his spine as he spoke the name. 'Never seen such a man! Looked like he'd had himself a fight with the Devil himself and lost! I've seen men mauled by cougars look better than he did!'

'But he brought her here!'

'Yep! Reckon you can't judge a book by its cover!'

'Iron Eyes!' Barker repeated the name. 'You said he was a bounty hunter! Yet he remained here throughout the surgery! Why would he do that?'

'I dunno!' Jackson rubbed his neck again. 'He seemed genuinely upset by your daughter being shot! There must be a heart buried inside his twisted carcass someplace! But he sure didn't want anyone to know about it!'

'I'd like to meet that man!' Barker said. 'Without his quick actions Holly would have probably died in that hotel! Do you think he'll return here?'

Jackson tilted his head and looked through his bushy eyebrows. 'Reckon he might return just to see how little Holly is doing! But be warned, he ain't no picture to look at!'

Barker moved closer to the window. He had

spotted something below. He raised a hand and pointed.

'Look! You were right! Men are carrying a body up here!'

Jackson sighed. 'I knew it! The bastard ain't dead! Good job I boiled up my instruments!'

Barker opened the door as four burly men reached the top of the steps. They carried the blood-soaked figure into the office and placed it on the crude table where the physician always did his surgery.

Jackson stepped closer to the motionless body. He then gasped in a mixture of shock and surprise. 'Sheriff Bodine!'

'Somebody shot the sheriff through his office window and stoved his head in, Doc!' one of the men said.

'We figure it was something to do with his prisoner!' another ventured. 'That critter's gone!'

Andrew Barker sat down beside his daughter. 'This is insanity!'

Jackson pressed three fingers against the sheriff's neck, then leaned over the man, who was barely alive.

'Chet?' Jackson said into the ear of the lawman. 'Can you hear me, Chet?'

There was no answer.

Duke Layne hauled rein. His exhausted mount

almost fell as it stopped beneath its master. The outlaw dropped to the ground and grabbed at its bridle. He started walking, pulling the weary animal behind him. The rocks were smooth and appeared like fresh-baked bread stacked high above the sand and brush. Layne was tired but knew that he had no time to waste. Slowly he managed to lead the horse up through the narrow gaps between the giant rocks. He had to reach the top of this stony outcrop to see if he had finally managed to shake off the deadly Iron Eyes.

After thirty minutes of soul-draining effort he saw and felt the morning sun as it rose up across the arid prairie to his left. Light swept like a tidal wave over everything until it found the weary outlaw and his mount. Layne pulled the brim of his hat down to shield his eyes and then quit walking.

Without realizing it he had reached the summit of the strange stack of rocks. He sat and stared down at the land below him. It stretched away for as far as he could see.

Fear had driven him on when he had recalled who was trailing him and his partner after they had slaughtered most of the people in the Silver Springs hotel. The gold coins he had stolen bulged in his pants pocket. It did not seem an awful lot for so much killing, but he and Craven had killed far more for a lot less in their time.

Even with the warmth of the morning sun on his bones, he still shook. The fear was still with him. The picture of Iron Eyes, seen over his shoulder a few days earlier, still burned into his thoughts.

The bounty hunter would not quit. They had managed to put distance between them and their lethal pursuer on several occasions during the long endless chase but Iron Eyes somehow managed to catch up with them every time.

Layne's eyes searched the ground below him. It was not the easiest of tasks. The overnight frost started to turn into mist as the sun's rays heated up the prairie. It was like looking into a vat of boiling stew.

The outlaw knew that splitting up was the smartest thing he and Craven had done since they had realized who was dogging their trail.

Even the infamous Iron Eyes could not chase two riders headed in different directions.

Or could he?

Layne was hungry. Hunger was chewing at his innards. He rose to his feet and opened the satchel of one of his saddle-bags. He pulled out a half-eaten chunk of jerky. He put it between his teeth and tore off a strip. His jaw ached as he ground up the dried beef between his teeth. His eyes continued their search for the man who wanted him and his partner dead.

45

Had the bounty hunter followed Craven instead of him?

He prayed so.

Then he saw dust.

Layne stopped chewing and screwed up his eyes. He strained to see what or who was kicking up the dust far below him.

Then he realized that it was two horsemen, not one. For a moment his heart began to beat normally once more. Two riders meant that it was not Iron Eyes. Iron Eyes rode alone, he told himself.

He sighed with relief.

He went to sit down again when he noticed something else. The riders might not be the man he feared but they were following his trail. Layne took another bite of his jerky.

But this time he could not chew.

Fear raced through him again.

Whoever the two men were, they were after him just as Iron Eyes had been after him. He could see them trailing his hoof tracks between the tangled brush. His heart began to pound like a hammer once more beneath his grubby shirt.

His mind raced. Where could he go to escape the ever-pursuing hunters? He knew that he had arranged to meet up with Craven at Drover's Gulch but now he doubted that he would ever reach his more devilish partner. For years it had been Craven who had done what little thinking they required to rob and kill. Now alone for the first time the notorious outlaw feared that he might be unable to shoot his way out of the trouble which was coming after him.

Layne tossed the jerky away and pulled the nervous mount towards him. He grabbed the saddle horn, threw himself atop the horse and dragged the reins to his chest. He poked his boots into the stirrups, spat and then spurred.

The exhausted animal responded.

Duke Layne headed back down through the maze of narrow dust trails that cut through the massive rocks. He knew that the stack of boulders was between himself and the pair of horsemen. It ought to slow them up enough for him to reach Drover's Gulch, he thought.

But would it?

Once again the outlaw was riding with fear on his shoulder.

FOUR

Even the sunrise could not make Drover's Gulch look any better than it had during the hours of darkness. The hotel room was small by any standards. Apart from the soft, wide bed only a worm-chewed dresser occupied the room. Iron Eyes was propped up against two well-filled pillows with his guns to either side of him a few inches from his bony hands. As always, he had slept with open eyes throughout the long night since leaving Dooley with a bottle of whiskey in his hand. The bottle was empty yet it had not helped the bounty hunter find a peaceful rest.

Iron Eyes stared at the threadbare drapes which hung across the window. Through a crack in one of the panes a draught moved the drapes gently as a breeze blew out in the street.

The sunlight had stirred him into movement. He sat up, dropped his long legs over the side of the mattress and pulled on his boots. His body had started to hurt of late. Even the softest of mattresses seemed unable to ease that constant nagging pain which haunted his pitifully thin frame.

Maybe it was the lead he carried from untended bullet wounds that was starting to poison him. Whatever it was, it still hurt and that pain made Iron Eyes even more dangerous.

He plucked his Bowie knife off the bed and slid it down into the neck of his right boot. The ice-cold steel blade felt good against his skin.

Iron Eyes stood and glared at the window. The drapes still fluttered. That annoyed the thin man. He stretched out his left hand, grabbed the lace and tore it down. Dust filled the room as the bounty hunter ventured closer to the dirty glass.

The previous night he had been talked out of simply killing Craven by the old-timer. At the time he had been angry about that but now began to think about Craven's partner. Duke Layne might have eluded him when the pair went their separate ways but the ruthless bounty hunter knew his prey.

If Matt Craven was hanging around Drover's Gulch there had to be a reason. The only reason Iron Eyes could think of was that he and Layne

49

had arranged to meet up here back on the trail the previous day.

A crooked smile stretched across his hideous features. Would Duke Layne make it easier for Iron Eyes and appear here?

The bounty hunter thought so.

It would be like a lamb to the slaughter.

Suddenly a knock at the door resounded in the room. Faster than a wildcat, Iron Eyes ignored his aching bones and pounced across the bed. He grabbed both loaded weapons and landed on the floor opposite the window. His thumbs dragged back both hammers.

From a crouching position he aimed at the door.

'Who is it?' he snarled.

'Dooley, Mr Iron Eyes!' came the muffled reply.

'You alone?'

'Yep!'

Iron Eyes rose to his full height and then moved towards the door. Both barrels were still aimed at its flaking paintwork. He used the barrel of the Navy Colt in his left hand to slide the bolt across before taking a step backwards.

'Come in!'

Cautiously, Buck Dooley pushed the door and felt his blood freeze in his veins when he saw the pair of matched Colts. He gulped and tried to smile but failed.

'You recall me, Mr Iron Eyes? I know we was both a tad drunk but—'

'Get in here!' Iron Eyes ordered.

Dooley obeyed.

Iron Eyes pushed the door back into its frame and rested his shoulder against it. He looked at the man before him. Buck Dooley tried to keep calm but it was hard when faced with a pair of cocked .38s. He cleared his throat and ran a finger along his bandanna.

'I come to warn ya!'

'About what?'

'About Klute Varney!'

Iron Eyes raised a scarred eyebrow. 'Who the hell is Klute Varney, Dooley?'

There seemed to be a nervousness in the older man's mien. He shuffled his feet and gestured with his hands as he spoke.

'You ain't heard of Klute?'

'Nope!'

'He got bounty on him!' Dooley told him. 'Look at this! I got it from the old sheriff's office!'

The bounty hunter watched as Dooley produced a Wanted poster from his pants pocket and waved it under his nose. Iron Eyes studied it carefully. The image was vague and could have looked like a hundred different men. The bounty was also low.

'You trying to get me interested in someone

51

worth only two hundred bucks, Dooley? I got more than that in cold coin in my pants!'

Dooley shook his head and returned the browned paper to his pocket. He was nervous. Real nervous.

'This poster is years old!' Dooley said. 'I know for a fact he's worth ten times that nowadays! But it ain't the money I'm talking about!'

'Then what?'

'Klute is kin to Craven!' Dooley muttered. 'Close kin!'

Iron Eyes pushed one of his pistols into his belt so that its grip poked out over the buckle. He stared hard at Dooley and tried to understand.

'So?'

'Klute got himself a dozen guns, boy!' Dooley tried to make this sound impressive. 'They runs both sides of the border and it's said that they have got themselves a real big stash of money some-place! Klute don't cotton to anyone who gets close to any of his boys in case they tells where it's hid! Savvy?'

At last Iron Eyes understood. 'OK! I savvy! But why are you so lathered up?'

'Klute intends killing you!' Dooley was sweating. 'He's got boys perched on top of buildings all along Front Street!'

Iron Eyes gave a brief laugh.

'I don't think Klute will get far with that

daydream, Dooley! Wherever they are, I'll kill them before they get spittle on their rifle sights!'

'I come here in good faith to warn ya, boy!' Dooley looked scared. 'I overheard them in the livery when I took ya horse there last night! Klute and Craven was plotting! You're a dead man if'n ya don't hightail it out of Drover's Gulch! Klute ain't a *hombre* to mess with!'

Iron Eyes stooped and picked his trail coat up from the floor. He slid it over his lean frame.

'I don't run away from no man! Backshooters included!'

'Not man! Men, boy! A dozen or more men!' Dooley went to the window and pointed into the street. 'They're waiting for ya, Iron Eyes! Ya gonna get bushwhacked for sure!'

Iron Eyes did not speak. He walked to the side of the fearful Dooley, stared out of the window and thoughtfully pulled a cigar from his shirt pocket. He pushed it between his teeth.

'I'll go get ya horse and bring it round back of the hotel, boy!' Dooley said. 'You gotta get out of town now before they cuts ya down!'

'Don't go getting my pony until I tells you! I'm going out through the front door of this hotel!' Iron Eyes said through a cloud of smoke.

'That's suicide!'

'No it ain't!' Iron Eyes corrected him. 'The Apache say I'm already dead, old-timer! If them

53

Injuns are right, how can these varmints kill me?'

'Are you loco?'

'Ain't all ghosts a tad loco, Dooley?'

FIVE

Iron Eyes walked slowly down the long flight of wooden stairs towards the hotel lobby. A few men lay in chairs sleeping off their individual hang-overs. Only the clerk was awake and propped up behind his small desk with a cup of coffee in one hand and a pipe in the other. The man sat upright when he caught sight of the hideous bounty hunter.

Tom Jenkins had not been on duty when Iron Eyes signed the register the previous night. He shook with fear as the tall figure reached the lobby and closed the distance between them. His fumbling fingers dropped his pipe on to the floor and he placed the cup down.

He tried to speak but could not.

'You got a scattergun behind that desk, mister?' Iron Eyes asked in a low drawl.

'Y-yeah!' the clerk replied fearfully.

Iron Eyes held out a hand. 'Give it to me!'

'B-but!'

'Now!'

Buck Dooley had remained a good few yards behind Iron Eyes but soon reached the desk when he saw the clerk about to make a big mistake and refuse the bounty hunter's request.

'Ya better give him ya scattergun, Tom!' Dooley advised.

'Yeah?' The clerk looked at Dooley with raised eyebrows. He, like so many of the older townspeople, recalled when Dooley had worn a star.

'He won't shoot ya!' Dooley added.

Iron Eyes snapped his fingers. 'I will if ya don't hand over that gun, Tom!'

'What you want it for?' the clerk asked as his shaking hands reached below the desk and produced the well-oiled scattergun.

'I got me some killing to do, Tom!' Iron Eyes snatched the gun and checked it. 'Now find some shells!'

The clerk found a full box of shotgun shells and handed them to the man who held his hefty weapon. He shook on his chair and watched as Iron Eyes pushed two cartridges into its twin barrels and then snapped it shut.

'Who ya gonna kill?'

'Anyone who tries to kill me!' came the blunt reply.

Dooley trailed Iron Eyes as he walked towards the open doorway. The bounty hunter emptied the rest of the shells into the deep right pocket of his trail coat and paused in the doorframe.

'See 'em, boy?' Dooley asked. His trembling index finger pointed up to the rooftops. 'I see three up there!'

'I see six, old-timer!' Iron Eyes corrected him.

'On the roofs?'

'Yep!' Iron Eyes chewed on his cigar. 'Look across the street at the store-front windows. See the reflections? Just like a row of mirrors!'

Dooley nodded. 'Damn! You sure know ya business!'

'There's two more men hid behind barrels across the street outside the feed store, Dooley!' Iron Eyes indicated with the barrel of the gun. 'Ain't all of them, though! I wonder where the others are hid?'

'None of them looks like Klute or Craven!' Dooley said, rubbing his chin.

'Figures!' Iron Eyes pulled the hammers back until both the scattergun's barrels were primed. 'Most outlaws are cowards and don't do their own killing! They find fools to do it for them!'

'There's too many of them, Iron Eyes! Even for you!'

'Maybe!'

Dooley looked up at the scarred face. 'Let me go

57

get ya horse, boy! There's still time for you to light out of Drover's Gulch!'

'If I know backshooters, they probably got the back of the hotel covered as well!' Iron Eyes stated. 'Ain't no point in even trying! Nope! This will only be finished one way!'

'I'll help ya!' Dooley said.

Like a general surveying a potential battlefield, Iron Eyes studied everything within view. His keen hunting brain had already worked out how he would tackle this problem.

'Nope!' Iron Eyes said. 'You'll get in my way! I fight alone! I always fight alone!'

'How come you're so dead-set on this fight, boy?'

'I want Craven and Layne! These varmints out there are in my way and that's dumb!'

'Craven and Layne must be worth an awful lotta dough for a man to take such a risk!' Dooley sighed.

Iron Eyes glanced at him.

'It ain't the bounty no more! Now it's personal! I'm gonna make them pay for what they done to someone back at Silver Springs! I'll make sure they never do it again!'

Dooley was about to ask what he meant when a deafening crescendo filled the street and bullets tore up the boardwalk a few feet from where Iron Eyes was standing. The bounty hunter pushed

58

Dooley to the floor and quickly ventured out on the the boardwalk.

Using the porch overhang as cover from the outlaws above him on his side of the street, Iron Eyes moved to the very edge of the boardwalk and emptied both barrels of the scattergun at the men hiding behind the stacked barrels opposite. Splinters exploded as the buckshot destroyed the barrels and the men hidden behind them. The dry wall suddenly went crimson as gore covered it.

Iron Eyes dropped on to his knees into the sand behind the hitching rail and water trough. He placed the weapon on the ground and pulled one of his Navy Colts from his belt. He fired three shots in quick succession and watched as two of the outlaws fell backwards and the third toppled off the high building. A cloud of dust rose when the body crashed into the weathered wooden over-hang before bouncing lifeless on to the street. Iron Eyes pushed the pistol back into his belt, picked up the scattergun and expelled both its steaming cartridges. His bony fingers pulled two fresh shells from his pocket and rammed them into the hot chambers. He stood and flicked his wrist. The gun snapped shut again.

He paused and stared at the store windows across the street for a few seconds. When he saw the reflections of the outlaws he stood and raced out into the centre of the street. He turned and blasted one barrel at two of them, then swung the gun to his right and fired the second deadly barrel.

A million splinters mixed with blood rained down into the street. Again Iron Eyes reloaded the heavy weapon as his metal-coloured eyes vainly searched for others.

'Where's this Klute critter hang out, Dooley?'

'The Five Aces!'

Iron Eyes nodded and ran in the direction of the saloon. As his long thin legs brought him to within twenty feet from the saloon's swing doors, he heard a familiar noise to his left. Five horsemen whipped their mounts and galloped out from a side street.

The wild-eyed horses drove over the bounty hunter, sending him cartwheeling across the sand. Klute and Craven fired down at the prostrate man as they spurred.

Bullets tore through the tails of his coat as Iron Eyes raised the scattergun at them and blasted both barrels. The last rider was torn apart. His shredded body rolled off the saddle and landed a few feet from the bounty hunter. Through narrowed eyes Iron Eyes watched as all four remaining outlaws continued to fire their guns wildly in all directions. The sound of breaking windows echoed all around Front Street.

Iron Eyes scrambled to his feet and drew both his Colts. He fired into the cloud of dust kicked up from the hoofs of the outlaws' mounts but instinctively he knew he had not found his targets.

The four horsemen turned their horses at the nearest corner and were gone.

Iron Eyes spat out the crumpled cigar from his bloody mouth and dropped both his guns into his deep pockets. He scooped up the scattergun from the sand.

He walked back towards the hotel. When he reached it he stopped and stared at the body crumpled by its open door.

'Damn it all! Why didn't ya stay down, Dooley?' Iron Eyes muttered. 'I told ya what would happen!'

A fiery rage was burning deep inside the bounty hunter's tortured soul. Only killing his chosen prey could extinguish its flames.

A blistering bullet cut through the morning air. Its red-hot taper passed within inches of the rider's face. Duke Layne swung the horse around and stared back in disbelief to the boulders, which cast a giant shadow across the trail. At first he could not see them. Then another two blasts came from the bounty hunters' rifles. This time they were closer.

Too close.

Layne felt the burning in his side. His body contorted up as his mount bucked hard. Somehow he managed to stay astride his animal long enough to see the huge hole a couple of inches above his belt. The bullet had taken not only a chunk of his coat and shirt but a lump of flesh from his body.

Blood flowed unchecked as the outlaw gripped the reins and pressed his spurs. Then he felt the impact below him. The horse gave a pitiful cry and crashed into the sand.

Layne rolled over and kicked himself free of the saddle which had pinned his left leg to the ground. His fingers clawed at the soft ground until he was again facing his two followers. He dragged his Winchester from its scabbard, then pushed himself up close to the blood-soaked saddle. He cocked the weapon and rested its long barrel on top of the twitching animal.

Two more shots cut into the fallen horse. Layne fired blindly and then pushed its trigger guard down once more to eject the bullet casing.

As he pulled the lever back up he heard them.

The horses were thundering towards him. Layne began to panic as he crawled to the neck of the horse. He squinted hard and saw them. Whoever the pair were, Layne had never seen them before.

Again he squeezed the trigger of the rifle.

This time the weapon kicked him backwards. He fell on his spine and then felt the agony of his wound as the sand filled the brutal cavity.

He attempted to rise but the horsemen were upon him. Their rifles were aimed down at him with frightening intent.

'Drop that carbine!' Snake Peters ordered.

Buffalo Benson dismounted and leaned over. He pushed the barrel of his Winchester into the outlaw's face.

'You heard him!'

Layne's fingers relaxed. The rifle fell on to the sand.

'Who are you?' Layne asked.

'Bounty hunters, boy!' Benson snarled.

'Where's Iron Eyes?' Layne heard himself ask.

Benson raised a boot and then pressed it down on the fallen man's neck. He leaned on it until he saw the tears fill the outlaw's eyes.

'Forget Iron Eyes!' Benson growled. 'Snake and me are the men you gotta worry about now!'

SIX

There were eight of them in total. Junaco Apache from far to the south, their skin baked until it was almost brown, with warpaint markings across their faces and arms. They came out of the heat haze like phantoms, stopped their ponies atop a sandy crest and silently watched the trio of white men fifty yards below their vantage point. It was Buffalo Benson who first saw them as he was about to kick the man he and Peters had staked out in the blistering sun.

The large bounty hunter gave his partner a sly glance and spoke from the corner of his mouth.

'We got us company, Snake!'

Peters's jaw dropped when he looked to where Buffalo Benson was staring. 'Apache!'

'Yeah!' Benson muttered.

'What you figure they want?'

'Scalps!'

64

'Damn it all!' Peters snarled. 'Just when we was getting this little bastard to spill the beans!'

Benson knelt beside the brutally tortured Duke Layne. He grabbed the outlaw's sweat-soaked hair and dragged his head up from the sand until both sets of eyes were locked on to each.

'You gonna talk?'

'Nope!' Layne spat defiantly. 'Ain't worth my getting on the bad side of Klute Varney! Kill me if ya like! Klute would do a damn sight worse if he found out I spilled the beans about his stash!'

Benson raised the outlaw's head even higher. He shook it with venom.

'See them, ya damn fool?'

'Barely!' Layne gasped as sweat and blood trickled into his eyes.

'Them's Apaches, Layne!' Benson told him. 'You ever tangled with Apaches? They make me and Snake seem like Sunday-school teachers! You want we should leave you here for them to finish the job? Or maybe you might tell us what we wanna know!'

'Which is it, boy?' Peters added. 'Tell us where Klute's got his money hid or we leave ya and head on after ya pal! Craven ain't gonna be so loyal! He'll talk!'

'Apaches got ways of killing that can take days, Layne!' Benson drooled. 'Mind you, it'll seem like years by the time they finish ya off! I've seen them varmints gut a man and then leave him to the vultures! Some things can be worse than dying!'

Layne closed his eyes. 'OK! I'll tell you! Just cut me free and I'll take you there if that's what you want!'

'Now ya seeing sense!' Benson pulled out his knife and slid its blade across the leather bonds. He hauled the pathetic outlaw off the ground and threw him at the horses. 'Get on that nag fast!'

Peters pulled his Winchester from its scabbard and cranked its mechanism into action. He waited until his companion had mounted before throwing himself on to his own saddle.

Benson gathered up his reins. 'You figure that they're gonna attack us, Snake?'

'Yep!' came the simple reply. 'They ain't painted up just to look pretty, Buffalo!'

Duke Layne pushed his boot toes into his stirrups and held tightly on to his reins. He wiped the bloody sweat from his face and saw the Indians clearly for the first time. His throat tightened.

'They *are* Apaches!'

Buffalo Benson dragged his horse's head back until the animal had turned full circle. He surveyed the terrain and felt his heart start to pound. There was plenty of cover but it was a quarter of a mile from where their horses nervously pawed at the ground with their hoofs. Brush and rocks capable of giving sanctuary to a hundred horses was within view but also within the range of the Apaches' arrows.

'Which way we headed, Buffalo?' Peters held his rifle across his lap with its barrel resting upon the saddle horn. His eyes never left the eight horsemen on the sandy rise.

'There!' Benson pointed to the rocks and brushland.

Peters eyes flashed at his partner. 'They'll cut us down for sure before we gets halfways there!'

'Not if you gives me and the kid plenty of cover!' Benson growled.

'What about me?' Snake Peters felt the hair on the nape of his neck start to tingle. 'I'm gonna be stuck here while you two ride into them bushes and rocks! I don't like it!'

'That's the way it's gonna be!' Benson snapped and reached across to the bridle of Layne's horse. His massive hand ripped the reins from the outlaw's grip. Without uttering another word, Benson spurred and started to ride towards the rocky outcrop with the outlaw in tow.

Peters felt his own mount shy as the two others thundered away. He steadied it and then saw the raised bows.

Arrows flew through the air. The whistling sound chilled the bounty hunter. He fired his Winchester. He just had time to see one of the Apaches fall from his pony before half the arrows tore into him and his horse.

A chilling death cry came from the horse.

Peters felt the animal crumple beneath his saddle. When it hit the ground he realized that one of the deadly projectiles had also found his flesh. He lay on the sand with his rifle in his hands. Pain ripped through him. His eyes focused on the arrow protruding from his guts. It was in deep. Too deep ever to be withdrawn without tearing out his innards.

The bounty hunter glanced to his side. He saw the two horsemen fleeing at pace towards the place he knew would protect them as more arrows landed all around his fallen body. Anger swelled inside him. He rose up on his elbow and pushed the rifle lever down and back up again. His finger curled around the trigger and he fired. Again his aim had been true. One of the young Apaches was punched off the back of his pony.

'I might be finished but I'm gonna take ya all to hell with me!' Peters vowed.

Then the sound of the Apaches' war chants filled his ears. It was a sound he had heard long ago and had never forgotten.

The riders tore through the dust and heat haze straight at him. He attempted to prime the rifle again but his strength seemed to be leaving him as fast as the blood which pumped from his stomach.

Peters dropped the hefty rifle, drew his Colt and

managed to pull its hammer back with his thumb. He blasted at the sound of the approaching warriors. Suddenly the unshod horses rode out of the dust and haze. Their masters forced the animals straight at the helpless bounty hunter.

The unshod hoofs crushed Peters' body deep into the sand. The Apaches continued on to chase Benson and Layne towards the distant rocks. Riding with their legs gripping and guiding the ponies' bodies, the Apaches used their bows to keep the arrows shooting at the pair ahead of them.

What was left of Snake Peters on the blood-splattered sand behind them, was dead.

SEVEN

Andrew Barker patted Doc Jackson on the back. He knew how hard and long the man had worked in a vain attempt to save the life of the sheriff. Blood still dripped on to the office floor as Jackson raised a hand and closed the lawman's eyes.

'You tried!' Barker said. 'I never seen anyone try as hard to save anyone, Doc!'

'Can't win 'em all!' Doc Jackson sighed regretfully. 'But I sure wish I'd won this one, Mr Barker!'

Barker looked at the doc's tired face and nodded. 'I know!'

'Me and old Chet have bin friends for more than twenty years, I guess!' Jackson continued. 'I brought both his young 'uns into the world! I tended his wife before the fever done for her!'

'Did he say who did this?' Barker asked as he sat down next to his still unconscious daughter.

Jackson looked straight at the businessman. 'He sure did! He said something about a man with that bounty hunter did this!'

'Bounty hunter?' Barker repeated the words. 'You don't mean Iron Eyes, do you?'

'Not Iron Eyes! He'd never do anything like this!' Jackson hastened to explain. 'I mean the dirty dog called Buffalo Benson! Him and his partner!'

Barker gave a sigh.

'I thought that bounty hunters were on the side of the law, Doc!'

'Some are! Some are worse than the vermin they hunt!' The doctor shrugged. 'Far worse!'

'So the sheriff told you who did this to him?' Barker seemed amazed.

'Yep! His words were faint but Chet said Benson's partner shot him, stove his head in and then bust the bastard out of the jail!' Jackson stared at his hands. They were coated in dried blood. His best friend's blood.

'This sort of thing would never happen back East!'

Thoughtfully Jackson moved to a small dresser upon which there was a bowl. He lifted a jug and poured water into the bowl. He picked up a well-used bar of soap and started to wash the evidence of his failure from his weathered flesh. 'But this ain't the East, Mr Barker! This is what some folks call the Wild West! A romantic name for a filthy place!'

Barker pulled out his wallet and opened it. It was filled with hundred-dollar bills. He spread them out like a fan. His eyes then looked up at the doctor.

'I hear that money can buy a posse!'

Jackson nodded. 'You figurin' on hiring some men to hunt down them bounty hunters?'

'Someone has to try and get justice for the sheriff!'

Jackson lifted a towel and dried his hands. 'You ought to leave that to someone who knows how to deal with vermin!'

'You mean Iron Eyes?'

'Yep!'

A cloud of arrows passed over the heads of the two riders. Benson pulled his reins back and threw himself to the ground as Layne's mount caught up with him. He reached up, hauled the outlaw from his saddle and dragged him into the bushes behind a giant boulder. The hefty bounty hunter pushed his shaking captive to the ground, then gathered up the reins of their mounts and tied them firmly to a branch. Then he hauled his Winchester from beneath his saddle.

'We're gonna get killed!' Layne said. He coughed.

'Not if I got anything to do with it, we ain't!' Benson answered. He ripped his saddle-bags from behind the cantle and tossed them down. He crouched, cocked the rifle into action and then started to fire.

'Give me a gun!' the outlaw begged. 'I'll help you fend them Apaches off!'

'Shut the hell up!' Benson growled between shots. 'Open them satchels and find me some ammunition!'

Layne's sweating hands fumbled with the metal buckles. 'I'm a good shot!'

'I don't intend letting you shoot me, Layne!' Benson said. He continued to empty his rifle magazine into the Apache riders, who were still thundering towards them.

Layne pulled out a box of shells. 'I got the rifle bullets!'

'Load it!' Benson pushed the rifle into the outlaw's hands, then drew his guns from their holsters.

Dust swirled between the braves and the two men behind the massive rocks, making it difficult to see the whooping Apaches. But Benson continued to fire one gun after another in a vain attempt to kill the riders.

More arrows bounced off the boulders.

Layne pushed one bullet after another into the rifle and then held it out towards the bounty hunter. 'Loaded!'

Benson tossed his guns at the outlaw and viciously grabbed the Winchester. 'Load my .45s!'

Layne found another box in the saddle-bags and opened it. He started to load the smoking guns. Each cartridge that he forced into the chambers made him think how easy it might be to turn the weapons on the creature who held him prisoner. Sweat dripped down his face as three of the Apaches' ponies passed by them without their riders.

'You must have killed a few of them!' Layne commented.

Buffalo Benson was not so sure. He could also sense that the six remaining Indians were far too smart to be cut down quite so easily. He stopped firing, tossed his guns down on the sand next to the outlaw and grabbed and cocked his rifle again.

'Why's it gone quiet?' Layne asked.

Benson raised himself up to his full height. He stood like a bear waiting to rip something apart. His eyes searched the rocks above them and the brush which had them hemmed in on three sides. Their horses became restless. They pulled at their tethers and started to paw their shod hoofs at the ground.

The bounty hunter moved between the animals. His every step was watched by the shaking outlaw, who reloaded the Colts.

Layne went to speak again when he saw

Benson's large hand rise and shake at him. The outlaw went silent.

Then all hell broke loose.

Suddenly the half-dozen Apache warriors made their presence known. Two had climbed up over the smooth rocks above them and readied themselves to pounce. Another pair of the heavily painted braves came from the right whilst the remaining two appeared from the left.

Bows unleashed their venom.

Knives glistened in the sun.

Arrows bore down on them. Knowing there was no time even to think, Benson started to fire his Winchester at the sounds of the Indians even before he could actually see them clearly.

Like a bolt of deadly lightning, an arrow came down from one of the warriors high above them and went through the left leg of the bounty hunter. Another landed within inches of the terrified outlaw. Benson screamed and then blasted his carbine upwards. His huge hands milked the mechanism and trigger of the well-oiled rifle as he sank slowly to his knees.

His shots were true. Both painted men fell heavily from their lofty perches and crashed to either side of Duke Layne. The outlaw swallowed hard and cocked the hammers of the guns he had just loaded for the burly bounty hunter.

Layne ignored the fear which had gripped him

75

like a hangman's noose. He stood and started to fire both handguns at the Apaches, who were almost on top of them.

The acrid taste of gunsmoke filled the air. Layne kept firing at the charging warriors as he saw the bounty hunter slump down between their two skittish horses.

The two braves to his right were hit. One fell on to his face whilst the other was knocked sideways. Then one of the Apaches crashed into him. Layne saw the flashing blade and tried to beat his attacker off.

The dagger thrust out and caught the outlaw high. He felt the blood flowing from his chest. He raised one gun. Then the other. His left trigger finger squeezed the last bullet from the pair of .45s. The Indian was blown a dozen feet backwards by the sheer force of the deadly bullet.

Pain ripped through Layne. The outlaw fell against the smooth rocks and gasped. His eyes darted all around him. As the smoke cleared Layne fell down beside the saddle-bags again. His fingers tried to reload the weapons but blood was everywhere.

It was his blood.

He dropped the guns and raised both hands to his chest. He felt the knife. It had been driven into him hard until only its hilt was exposed. Blood pumped with every beat of his heart through his fingers.

'Benson!' Layne shouted. 'I think I'm done for!'

'Good! Saves me a job!' The snarling bounty hunter tore off his bandanna and tied it around his thigh as tightly as he could. He then ripped the arrow from his leg and screamed at the heavens.

'Benson!' Layne called out again.

Benson looked up through screwed-up eyes. To his horror he saw the pair of guns aimed straight at him. His face twitched as anger overwhelmed him. His fingers went for the rifle lying on the sand beside him.

The two bullets that came from the guns in Layne's hands stopped them from reaching their goal. Benson glared at the outlaw furiously. Suddenly the big man realized that the tables had turned.

'I reloaded them again, Benson!' Layne smirked through his own agony.

'What you doing, you little squirt?'

'I'm thinking of killing you, you fat stinking bastard!' Layne replied.

Buffalo Benson glanced at his own wound and then across at Layne's. Both were pumping blood as though there was no tomorrow. He knew that for at least one of them there would indeed be no tomorrow.

Silently he wondered which one of them would die first.

The bounty hunter was taking no bets.

77

Even with darkness only an hour away and shadows stretching across their trail the rider and horse thundered through the unfamiliar land at top speed. Iron Eyes gave little if any thought for the fresh mount beneath him. He drove his spurs into its flesh and whipped its shoulders mercilessly, trying to force the sweating mount to increase its pace. The horse had not come cheap and had cost most of what little money the bounty hunter had left in his deep pockets, yet he still treated it the same way as he treated all his mounts.

With contempt.

Iron Eyes showed it no mercy. To him it was just another of his tools to use any way he saw fit. Apart from a handful of thin black cigars and two bottles of whiskey, Iron Eyes had given no thought to provisions when he had abruptly departed from Drover's Gulch.

He was used to the pain of hunger and relished it for making him even meaner than he normally was. It made him want to kill anything or anyone who got between him and the bounty money he could almost smell.

Yet there was an urgency in him now that was totally alien to his make-up. He was in a rush to catch up with Klute Varney and his men. Not just for the prices on their heads but the taste he knew would fill him with pleasure once he dispatched them the the fiery bowels of Hell.

It was the taste of vengeance.

Iron Eyes spurred and whipped the hapless animal up a steep sandy ridge as though his very life depended upon his reaching its top. When he reached the flattened area he brutally stopped the horse and dropped to the ground.

He had seen the tracks of the men who had fled Drover's Gulch leading to the right of the unstable sandy hill but knew that if he were to see any clue as to which direction they were headed, he had to find himself a high enough perch.

Iron Eyes had found it.

Like an eagle floating on a thermal of hot air, the bounty hunter stood beside his animal and studied everything below him.

It did not take long for his keen eyesight to spot the outlaws' dust.

Even the trees and brush could not keep the secrets of riders in this dry terrain. Dust cut up through the tree canopies and caught the rays of the dying sun.

He pulled a cigar from his trail coat pocket, lit it and sucked in the strong smoke. Once his airways were filled with the acrid smoke he relaxed.

To him it was obvious where the riders were headed. He could see a river ahead of the trail dust and beyond the river a sod-built house, illuminated by the setting sun.

He knew that now all he had to do was wait and watch. Only when the outlaws reached their destination would he continue his own ride.

Continue his unrelenting hunt.

Iron Eyes exhaled. A line of smoke drifted from his gritted teeth. He had plenty of time.

EIGHT

The four men inside the small cabin were nervous. Even with the pot-belly stove filling the sod structure with warmth and a hot meal inside their guts, each of them was still uneasy. For each of them knew that they should have finished Iron Eyes off when they had had the chance. Yet if the infamous bounty hunter was only half as good as his reputation claimed they knew there was more chance of them joining their fellow outlaws on a one-way journey to Hell, not Iron Eyes.

For nearly a decade Klute Varney had earned his name as a fast draw and one of the cleverest outlaws along the border. Yet even he found it impossible to settle down and rest. The sight of the notorious Iron Eyes had branded itself into his mind. It would remain there for eternity.

Matt Craven was probably the least jumpy of the four outlaws as they sat around the rickety table

81

and stared at the tin plates before them. He had known the horror of being hunted down by Iron Eyes and now, back with his leader and two of Varney's best guns, he felt safer than he had done for weeks.

Clu Jones and Frog Kettle said nothing. They too had stared at the bounty hunter close up when they had driven their horses past his skeletal form. His image refused to quit their thoughts.

Silence filled the cabin.

Yet for all the quietness, the four men showed no signs of bedding down for the night.

Each of them knew that Iron Eyes would not give up easily.

He would follow.

It was not in his nature to quit. The question each of them silently shared was: when would Iron Eyes show? And when he did, how would he make his play?

It mattered little to Iron Eyes whether he was still in Texas or had crossed the unmarked border into Mexico. Man-made borders meant nothing to the bounty hunter. He went where the tracks of his prey led him.

Where their scent betrayed them.

Iron Eyes pulled back on his reins and felt the tired animal beneath him slow to a stop. His keen eyes required little help from the bright moon which had replaced the burning sun. He just knew where the four outlaws were.

The sod structure blended into the background well. No light escaped from its wooden shutters or doorjamb but the smoke from its chimney had led the bounty hunter straight to it anyway.

He sat motionless atop the weary horse. A thousand times he had been in a similar situation. His mind raced as the night breeze moved his long mane of black hair. Now it was down to killing.

Killing creatures who deserved the justice he was willing to dish out. He wondered how much they were all worth. He had paper for only Craven and Layne in his pockets, that came to a princely sum. He knew that Klute Varney and the two other riders had to be worth more. A lot more.

His only problem was finding a town where he might be able to collect the reward money before his prey rotted. He knew that Silver Springs was a long ride away but it had law and the ability to pay him for his hard work.

Iron Eyes had started out chasing two wanted souls but now found he had a quartet of outlaws trapped. A crooked smile crossed his lips.

There was profit here. He could smell it as clearly as he could smell the smoke that drifted down from the blackened chimney stack.

Silently he slid down to the ground. His long thin legs absorbed the shock of the impact in well-rehearsed action.

The bounty hunter studied the area.

The outlaws' four horses had been unsaddled and tethered to the rear of the soddy. That pleased Iron Eyes. It meant there was no quick escape for any of them.

It took a long time even for well-practised men to saddle a horse in the best of situations. This was not going to be the best of situations for those he sought. It would be all they could manage to do just to remain alive under his onslaught.

Iron Eyes grabbed his reins and secured them to a large rock at his feet. He knew that even the most faithful of horses shied when the shooting started. This creature, that he had spurred and whipped mercilessly, would run for sure when the first shot was fired given half a chance. The tall bounty hunter would not risk losing his mount in this remote land. He opened one of the flaps of his saddle-bags and pulled out a whiskey bottle. Three inches of the fiery liquor remained. He tore its cork from the bottle neck and spat it away.

He would not require it again.

Holding the bottle to his thin, scarred lips, Iron Eyes tilted his head back and started to swallow the liquor. It did not take long for most of the bottle's contents to be consumed. Most but not all.

Iron Eyes stopped when there was a mere half-inch of whiskey left in the bottle.

His eyes flashed briefly at the cabin, then returned to the bottle in his bony hand.

He had an idea.

He placed the bottle on top of the rock, then pulled out the tail of his well-worn shirt. He tore a strip from it and then stuffed the fabric into the neck of the bottle.

Iron Eyes shook the bottle until the shirt strip was soaked in the powerful liquor. Again a smile came over his features.

He slid the bottle into his right coat pocket and pushed a cigar between his lips. He struck a match and lit the long black weed. He drew deeply until the cigar was well alight. He tossed the match away and started for the cabin.

As he went he pulled one of his matched guns from his belt and cocked its hammer.

His long stride ate up the ground beneath his boots. The distance closed between the bounty hunter and the sod cabin quickly.

The Grim Reaper's closest rival was about to fight. Only death could stop him.

NINE

Three hours earlier, amid the carnage of the six dead Apaches and the blood-soaked sand which surrounded them, two violent men had faced one another with only one thought between them. The death of the other.

The bounty hunter versus the outlaw. A confrontation which would continue until one of them made an error. For hours neither man would do so.

As the last rays of the sun had cast their bright splintered light across the sand between Buffalo Benson and himself, Duke Layne made a mistake.

Just one small mistake. It had proved to be his first and last since being captured by the fearsome bounty hunter.

Layne had blinked and given his foe a few precious seconds in which to make his move. Benson was too seasoned to miss what he knew might be his only chance.

Somehow he had managed to ignore his own agonizing wound, lift himself up off the ground between their two horses. He had thrown his full weight at the outlaw. His sheer bulk had overwhelmed Layne.

Benson had torn both guns from Layne's bloody hands, grabbed his prisoner's throat and pinned him against the smooth boulder.

All, it seemed to his victim, in the time it had taken to blink.

In the following five minutes the resourceful bounty hunter had managed to learn everything he needed to know about the outlaw leader Klute Varney.

And the whereabouts of Varney's legendary fortune.

A few seconds before he snapped Layne's neck Benson had been told where Varney's fabulous stash of money was hidden south of the border. Benson recognized the description of the hideaway. He had been there many times in his search for other men with prices on their heads.

Within the next five minutes Buffalo Benson had slid his guns back into their holsters, draped the outlaw's lifeless body over the saddle of his horse and secured it. He then mounted his own horse and set off on his quest.

Before the sun had set Buffalo Benson had

ridden past the bodies of the fallen Apache braves, which were scattered all around the small rocky area. He gave no thought to his lifeless partner and rode on. The body of Snake Peters would have to await the dawn and the vultures which would pick its bones clean.

Benson spurred his mount and led the outlaw's horse with its valuable cargo south. He knew that the terrified Duke Layne had told him the truth as to the whereabouts of Varney's fortune.

The bounty hunter knew when dying men were lying.

It was all in the eyes.

TEN

It was far darker at the rear of the small sod cabin. Shadows gave cover to the tall thin man in the long trail coat as he silently made his way around the four tethered horses, making sure he always remained downwind of them. Iron Eyes knew that he carried the scent of death upon him and that that acrid aroma spooked all animals, especially horses.

His first thought had been to kick the cabin door in and just start shooting. But advancing years had taught him that sometimes it was wiser to try and out-think your prey. His body ached from the many wounds he had received over the years of hunting two-legged animals. Most of their lead had been cut out of his thin body, but not all. Some outlaws' bullets had gone too deep for even the most skilled of surgeons to find. They remained inside him and slowly poisoned his pitiful being.

Iron Eyes moved to the back wall and studied it. He pushed his Navy Colts into his belt and then reached up. His fingers found the wooden shingles and gripped them. Iron Eyes gripped the still smoking cigar between his teeth, mustered all his strength and pulled himself up as quietly as he could until he was able to throw his left leg over the overhang.

Iron Eyes rested for a few seconds and studied the rooftop upon which he lay. It looked dried and worm-eaten but he knew that his frame was far lighter than that of most men of his height. The roof could take his weight.

Slowly he rose and carefully edged his way to the rusted chimney stack that protruded from the shingles. Smoke drifted out from it and was blown away quickly on the night air. Iron Eyes nodded to himself and then tore what was left of his shirt from his body. The fragile fabric was so brittle he did not have to remove his coat.

Iron Eyes carefully stuffed the torn shirt into the top of the chimney until it was completely blocked. He knew it would be a few moments before the smoke backed up and started to feed out from the stove inside the cabin.

After taking the whiskey bottle from his pocket Iron Eyes started to walk carefully down the slight incline towards the front of the cabin. He moved as quietly as he could.

Klute Varney replaced the coffee pot on top of

the stove and slowly looked up at the wooden ceiling. A sprinkling of dust drifted down from between the dry rafters close to where the chimney stack went out of the cabin's roof.

Varney waved a hand at his seated cohorts and then pointed a finger upward before silently removing one of his guns from its holster and priming it for action.

The three other outlaws pulled their weaponry and cocked the hammers as Varney walked towards the table and leaned over them.

'That's either vermin up there or we got us a visitor!'

Matt Craven's face went ashen. 'Iron Eyes?'

'It's gotta be him!' Varney said firmly. 'Who else would be loco enough to take us on?'

'Look!' Frog Kettle whispered.

They all looked. The dust was moving towards the front of the cabin. Even though they could not hear him, they knew that the notorious hunter of men was up there.

Clu Jones rose to his feet and pointed the barrel of his gun at the black pot-belly stove. Smoke was starting to billow out from its open door.

Varney nodded knowingly. 'The damn bastard's blocked up the stack! He's trying to choke us out of here!'

'I ain't leavin' here, Klute! He'll kill us for sure!' Craven said.

Varney continued to look to where the dust drifted from the rafters. 'I thought you said he was smart, Matt! Only a fool would try and round us up by getting on the roof!'

Now all four men were standing. They knew that the man they had encountered back at Drover's Gulch was here. Smart or loco, he was here.

More smoke billlowed into the room.

'We'll choke to death if we stay in here!' Jones warned the others.

Varney gritted his teeth and kept staring at the ceiling. He was trying to work out exactly where the bounty hunter was and what he might do next.

Craven gripped Varney's arm. 'It has to be Iron Eyes, Klute! He's out to suffocate us!'

'Easy!' Varney pushed his nervous companion away and edged closer to the door. He placed an ear against the sod wall and listened. He knew that even the slightest vibration would give him an idea where their hunter was. The trouble was that Iron Eyes had stopped moving. There was no sound.

The smoke was now choking them. Their eyes were streaming as their lungs fought for air.

'We gotta make a break for it, Klute!' Kettle said.

'Frog's right!' Jones coughed.

'Not yet!' Varney raised his guns and aimed them upward. 'First we gotta make that bastard dance!'

All four men held their breath and trained their

weapons on to the ceiling. Bullets tore through the wood over their heads with ferocious accuracy. The outlaws squeezed their triggers and fanned their gun hammers until they fell on empty chambers. Without the slightest hesitation they all reloaded and were ready for even more action.

'We must have gotten him!' Kettle exclaimed.

'Why didn't we hear him fall?' Craven whispered. 'We should have heard him fall!'

On the roof Iron Eyes stood a mere foot away from the shattered roof shingles. His eyes narrowed with fury. He lifted the bottle to his face. The cigar in his teeth touched the liquor-sodden cloth in the bottle's neck. The cloth ignited. Iron Eyes leaned over the edge of the roof, drew his arm back and aimed at the door.

'C'mon! Let's teach Iron Eyes he's taken on more than even he can chew this time!' Varney dragged the door towards him. Cold air rushed into the cabin. Just as he went to step out something came down from the roof. The whiskey bottle and its burning rag stopper smashed at the outlaws' feet. A curtain of fire briefly forced them back. Flames raced up the sod wall and ate at the dry timber doorframe.

'He's a madman!' Jones exclaimed.

Shielding his face from the heat, Varney kicked sand from the cabin floor at the liquor-fuelled flames, while Kettle used his vest to beat the blaze into submission. Within seconds they had extinguished it.

Furiously Varney swung his guns upward and trained them on to the ceiling. His shots tore through the already splintered woodwork.

'Now! Let's get him!' Varney yelled to his three followers. All four ran out into the darkness. Each of them turned and started to fire blindly through the smoke at the roof directly above the cabin door.

As the swirling smoke thinned the outlaws stared in disbelief to where they had aimed their combined venom. There was no sign of the bounty hunter.

'Where is he?' Craven screamed out as terror gripped him.

None of the others answered. There was no clue to where Iron Eyes was. The only certainty was that he was not up on the rooftop as they had imagined. Fearfully, the four outlaws closed in on the cabin. Their guns darted from one shadow to another in frantic search of the man they wanted to kill before he killed them.

Varney waved a gun at Kettle and Jones. 'Saddle our horses fast, boys! We're getting out of here tonight!'

The pair of nervous outlaws rushed to the frightened animals, dragged blankets and saddles from the fence pole and feverishly began to ready the quartet of horses.

Craven was still scared. Now all the stories he had heard about Iron Eyes had returned to his troubled mind. He shook with uncontrollable dread.

'Where is he, Klute?'

'Easy, Matt!' Varney ordered. 'He's around here someplace!'

Craven felt his heart pounding hard against his shirt. He was panting like a hound on the scent of a racoon.

'I told ya that he ain't human!' Craven stammered. 'He's dead, like the tales say! We can't beat him, Klute! No one can get the better of him! Ya can't kill a dead man! Nobody can kill a dead man! It ain't possible! We're just notches waiting for him to carve on to his gun grip!'

'Shut up, you yella dog!' Varney lashed out. He hit Craven across the face with the barrel of one of his guns and watched the startled outlaw stumble and then stare at him like a frightened rabbit. 'He's no different from any other back-shooting bounty hunter! He can die! If he shows himself, I'll prove it!'

Craven rubbed the blood from his cheek with the back of his shirtsleeve and followed his leader to the roof overhang. He watched as Varney holstered one of his guns and ran his fingers down the sod wall near the smouldering doorframe.

'What is it?' Craven asked.

'Blood!' Varney replied. 'Dead men don't bleed, Matt!'

'Blood?' Craven stepped closer. He then saw the blood on Varney's fingertips glisten in the moonlight. His head swung around. 'But where'd he go, Klute?'

'He high-tailed it out of here like all wounded critters!'

Jones and Kettle led the four horses to the two men.

'If'n he's wounded, are we gonna finish him off?' Craven asked.

'Are you plumb loco?' Varney grabbed his reins from Jones, stepped into his stirrup and mounted his horse. 'We're riding just like I said!'

The three others dragged themselves on to their horses beside their leader. Each of them sat with reins in one hand and a gun in the other.

'Where we going, Klute?' Kettle asked.

'To Devil's Canyon and our loot!' Varney said. He rammed his spurs into the sides of his mount. 'Reckon it's time for us to split our money and head our separate ways! Things are getting too damn hot around these parts!'

The four horsemen thundered away from the cabin. None of them looked back. If they had they would have seen the wounded Iron Eyes staggering from the rear of the sod structure. Holding his left arm with his bony fingers as blood poured between them the tall figure paused and leaned against the cabin for a few seconds.

'Devil's Canyon, huh?' Iron Eyes repeated the words he had heard Varney utter in a low drawl. 'So that's where ya headed! Better ride like quicksilver cos I know where that is and when I've dug this bullet out of my arm I'm coming after you, boys!'

Iron Eyes pulled the Bowie knife from the neck of his boot and made his way into the cabin. He dragged a chair across the floor, sat down beside the stove, then rammed the blade of the knife into the stove's hot embers. When it was red-hot he would use it to cut the bullet from his arm.

The smoke which billowed from the stove did not bother the bounty hunter. All he could think about was the four fleeing outlaws and the prices on their heads.

He knew he had made a mistake.

He vowed that he would not repeat it.

ELEVEN

Dawn came swiftly to the prairie. Its light illuminated the carnage to the eyes of the bareback riders who had steered their unshod ponies between the rocks to make their gruesome discovery.

The morning sun revealed the bodies scattered around the outcrop of boulders. Vultures had already swooped upon the slain Indians and started to feast upon their flesh before the thirty Apaches rode their ponies towards them.

These, unlike the slain Apaches, were the tribe's elders. They were all that was left of the Junaco Apache warriors who had roamed these lands since time itself had begun.

Herinaco had been chief for his entire adult life. Twenty-eight years of trying to stay one step ahead of the white intruders had aged him, though. Like the rest of his followers his black hair had become flecked with white.

The young men of his tribe lay strewn across the blood-soaked sand before them.

He pulled the mane of his white pony and stopped it. His followers surrounded him as he stared down at the eight bodies of their youngest braves.

The chief looked heavenward and screamed. It was the most chilling sound to have filled the ears of his braves in any of their lives. If a broken heart could be audible it would have sounded just like that pitiful outburst.

The braves slammed their bows against their shields until the vultures were frightened away from their feasting. The huge birds lifted off the ground and flew upward. They did not go far though. They perched upon tree branches and boulders and waited for another chance to swoop down and continue their gorging.

Herinaco dropped to the ground and walked from one body to the next. Each step ripped at his heart. At last he found the one he was looking for. He fell on to his knees beside it.

His son had been fourteen.

He would not get any older.

The rest of his warriors dismounted and slowly walked around the area, trying to identify the bodies which had been torn to shreds by the vultures' beaks and talons.

Herinaco slid his arms beneath the body of his only child and lifted him off the red sand. A chill filled his soul. He turned and walked towards his men.

Every eye was upon him.

'See the hoof marks, my brothers?' Herinaco bellowed. 'This is the work of white eyes! See how they slay mere children? Mere children armed with only bows and arrows. We shall honour our dead and then we shall follow the trail left by the animals that did this! But we shall not be armed with bows and arrows! We shall use our rifles!'

The Apaches raised their arms and began to chant.

'Many moons ago Cochise allowed the white eyes to enter our land! He was a woman who let them take and kill! He was fooled by the soft words and broken promises! I, Herinaco, am Apache! Now I will show them what it means to be Apache!'

The braves chanted even louder.

Herinaco had declared war.

Iron Eyes was hurt. Yet pain had not stopped his relentless pursuit of the outlaws who were driving their mounts further and further south. The low sun was hot and as it slowly crept up through the blue, cloudless sky, it grew hotter. The bedraggled horse beneath him was soaked in its own sweat and yet it still galloped as the cruel sharp spurs were driven into its flesh over and over again.

Devil's Canyon lay ahead, just over the next peak. The bounty hunter had been there many times during his unremitting search for men wanted dead or alive. A decade earlier he had discovered a short cut into the treacherous canyon that entailed riding over the high ragged crest of a sun-bleached mountain range. It had proved to be a route which allowed him to get the dead carcass of his prey back to civilization before it rotted under the blazing sun and became unrecogniz-able. It was pointless bringing the corpse of a wanted man to the law and claiming the reward on a face that no longer resembled its Wanted poster.

This was no trail for the faint of heart. Sheer drops to either side of the ruthless rider made it a dangerous place but Iron Eyes was unafraid. Death was no stranger to him. He cared little for life and had long forgotten what fear tasted like.

Iron Eyes stopped his horse beside a small pool of mountain water. It was fed from an even higher place. He dropped to the ground and sighed heav-ily. He held his reins and watched as the horse drank feverishly. Pain racked his emaciated body and his left arm throbbed like a war drum beneath his trail coat. Sweat traced from his hair and navi-gated the multitude of scars which adorned his face.

The bullet had been easy enough to dig out but

the scar tissue on his pitifully thin arm had been harder to mend. He had tried to use the hot blade of his knife to seal the wound but failed. He had then resorted to sewing his flesh with catgut. The skin had been weak and resisted even this. Blood still trickled down his arm and found its way to his bony hand.

Iron Eyes removed a bottle of whiskey from his saddle-bags and pulled its cork with his teeth. He shook his arm free of the coat sleeve and poured some of the liquor over the angry wound. It burned like fury but the bounty hunter refused to acknowledge its pain. He took two long swallows and then pushed the cork back into the neck of the bottle.

A rage was burning in him along with the brewing fever. He had somehow been bettered by the outlaws and was furious. No one had ever managed to get the better of him like this before. A million thoughts raced through his mind.

Was he getting old? Were his hunting skills now slipping away from him?

Had he finally met his match in Klute Varney?

Then his clouded thoughts saw the image of the small girl he had rescued from the blood-soaked hotel. He recalled her little white body as the doctor had operated on her and removed the deadly bullets.

There had been a time when such things would

THE REVENGE OF IRON EYES

have meant nothing to the dedicated killing machine called Iron Eyes. He could not understand why the small child kept returning to his thoughts.

All he knew for certain was that he had become angrier than ever before when he had discovered her in the carnage of the hotel's once pristine foyer.

Why?

He did not know her! Why was he so angry?

Iron Eyes slid the bottle back into its hiding-place and buckled up the satchel flap. He pulled on his coat again and rubbed his eyes, trying to clear the fog from them. In a desperate attempt to reclaim his thoughts he lit another cigar. He inhaled deeply and shook his head.

The constant pain dulled slightly. He did not know whether it was the whiskey or the smoke which had helped. All he knew was that he was still angry.

So angry that he was now more dangerous than he had ever been before. The fever and the pain mixed in with the rage had made him want to kill the four outlaws so badly it overwhelmed everything else inside his thin frame. He told himself it was for their combined bounty money but knew in reality it was far simpler.

It was for revenge.

He staggered a few steps and stared down into

103

the canyon. He stood there with the smouldering cigar hanging from his cracked lips. This was Devil's Canyon. It had been well-named.

Where in that labyrinth could they be? The question kept filling his mind.

It was impossible for him to see anything clearly down there as the heat haze rose to greet the ever-rising sun.

He knew the canyon well but had not been into it for at least five years. If Klute Varney had a secret hiding-place, it was new and it might be hard to find.

He had not attempted to follow their trail this time as they had left him for dead back at the cabin.

This time he was using his knowledge of the area to guide him to the place where, he had overheard Varney telling his cohorts, they were headed.

He had made good time taking the mountain trail. He knew that however clever the leader of the outlaws was, he did not know of the hazardous short cut.

Although Iron Eyes had wasted more than an hour tending to his wound after the outlaws had ridden off for Devil's Canyon, he knew that it was time he could afford to lose. The short cut was not obvious to most riders who came this way. He had only discovered it by accident.

If his calculations were correct, he should be

ahead of them.

Iron Eyes pulled on the reins and drew the tired animal to him silently. Then he spotted something far below.

Dust.

He raised a hand to shield his eyes from the brightness and forced himself to focus.

The four riders were heading into the jaws of the canyon.

Iron Eyes knew that as long as they remained in view he would see exactly where their hideout was. He was just about to sit down on a rock on the very edge of the high precipice when he spotted more dust to his left, further up the canyon. Whoever this was, Iron Eyes concluded, he was a good hour ahead of the outlaws.

His eyes narrowed as he tried to see through the swirling hot air which was getting thicker in the canyon as it grew hotter amid the sand-coloured rocks.

The rider must have set out long before either the outlaws or Iron Eyes to have gotten so far up into the canyon, the bounty hunter told himself.

Iron Eyes spat his cigar out and screwed up his eyes until they were almost shut. He was fighting not only the heat haze down on the floor of the canyon but the fog inside his fevered head.

At last his eyes obeyed him and focused upon the things he was straining to see. It was a rider leading a packhorse. Something was tied to the back of the packhorse and it wasn't provisions.

It was a body.

The birds circling above the horses told him that it was not just a body. It was a ripe one.

'Who the hell are ya?' Iron Eyes muttered angrily. 'Who are ya, damn it?'

Then he knew the answer and straightened up.

Perhaps it was the fringed jacket or the hat he recognized or just the way the rider sat his mount. Whatever it was, Iron Eyes knew who he was staring at from his lofty perch high on the ragged peak.

'Buffalo Benson!' he snarled. 'How the hell did you get here, you back-shooting bastard?'

TWELVE

The blazing sun was nearly directly overhead. Heat rose from the rocks and created a shimmering pool of air across Devil's Canyon, which obscured almost everything from the injured bounty hunter's weary eyes. Crumbling rocks slipped from beneath the shod hoofs of the tall horse as it blindly obeyed its master and slowly descended the the steep trail down into the canyon. They descended from the narrow trail down into the abyss.

But Iron Eyes did not notice. He was oblivious to the danger only inches away from his mount's hoofs. Even though he swayed from side to side on his saddle as pain racked his body he continued to spur the horse on.

He wanted to finish what he had started and he could only achieve that by getting down to the floor of the canyon and facing those he hunted.

It was nearly noon and not the best time of day to enter the canyon. Night offered protection from the blinding sun but noon offered no hiding-place. But he pressed on regardless.

All Iron Eyes could think of was catching up with the riders he had watched disappear into the widest of the many ravines which made up the notorious Devil's Canyon. He wanted revenge for what they had done to him. But most of all he wanted to get his hands on Matt Craven and punish him for what he had done to the innocent child Holly Barker back at Silver Springs.

He was halfway down when something alerted his dulled senses and caused him to stop his mount.

Iron Eyes raised a hand to shield his face from the bright sun. He stared out across at the golden-coloured peaks opposite him. For a moment he was not sure that his eyes were telling him the truth. They had lied to him so many times since he had been shot.

Then it became clear that it was exactly what he thought it was. Plumes of smoke were rising heavenward.

War smoke. That meant only one thing.

'Injuns!' Iron Eyes gasped.

His confused mind tried to work out what was happening. He had four outlaws somewhere below his high vantage point, whom he was about to take on, and then there was the mystery of Buffalo Benson and what he was doing in this unholy place.

Now there were Indians sending up war smoke and Iron Eyes knew that there was only one tribe of Indians capable of surviving in this hostile terrain.

Apaches.

And Apaches hated him more than he hated them.

Why were they sending smoke signals across the canyon top to one another? he silently asked himself. Had they spotted him on his long trek to this savage land? Perhaps they wanted to lay their hands and tomahawks on the outlaws as much as he wanted to blast them into Hell.

Maybe it was Buffalo Benson they wanted.

So many questions.

So few answers.

Iron Eyes pulled his Winchester from its scabbard and checked that it was fully loaded. It was. He rested it across his saddle horn and pulled his matched Navy Colts from his belt. He discarded spent shells, then reloaded the empty chambers with fresh .38s from his deep pockets. Once loaded he slipped one gun into each of the trail coat pockets. He licked his dry cracked lips and then tapped his spurs again.

The horse continued its way down the trail to

the floor of the canyon. Iron Eyes leaned back and allowed the animal to find its own route. The sound of the loose gravel kicked aside by his horse masked all other noises.

For the first time in a long while the bounty hunter was uncertain of what he was taking on.

Even on a bad day Iron Eyes knew he could get the better of Buffalo Benson. The outlaws had proved to be far more troublesome than he had thought possible, though.

The blood which trickled from his arm was proof of that. They were dangerous and he could not afford to underestimate them again.

To do so was to die.

As Iron Eyes approached the level ground his thoughts centred on only one of the problems that faced him. That was the Apaches and what they might do. He glanced upward as he stood in his stirrups and steadied his mount. Even through the thickening haze he could still see the smoke high above him.

It rose in well-crafted plumes. He wished he could read its ominous message.

Iron Eyes knew that trouble was coming, though.

For the first time he wondered if he were ready for it.

Klute Varney reined in and fought with his anxious

mount as his three cohorts swung their own horses around to an abrupt stop. The outlaw leader pointed up to the jagged peaks to their left and the smoke signals rising from its highest point. An unseen Apache brave high above them was sending his messages right across the numerous ravines carved out by a million years of time, which had become collectively known by the name of Devil's Canyon.

'Injun smoke!' Varney yelled to his companions.

The three others said nothing. They just watched fearfully as the smoke continued to drift into the midday sky. Even the dumbest of them knew that when Indians started talking with smoke it was serious.

Deadly serious.

Varney steered his horse between that of Craven and Jones and pointed far behind them. They could see the anxiety etched into his features. They turned and looked to where his eyes were aimed.

'Look! Another smoke signal!' he exclaimed.

Kettle held his reins tightly. 'Apaches!'

'Yeah, it's gotta be Apaches, Frog!' Varney agreed. 'They're the only Injuns that can live in this damn desert!'

'What they want?' Craven asked. Sweat ran down his face from his hatband and dripped on to his already wet shirt.

'I ain't sure!' Varney rubbed the trail dust from his face and frowned. He'd seen a lot of Indian smoke in his time south of the border and knew it usually meant trouble. Apaches didn't go to the trouble of making smoke unless there was something or someone they wanted dead.

'Do ya figure they're talking about us, Klute?' Jones asked.

'Could be, Clu!' Varney conceded. 'This is their land and we are trespassing, after all! I don't want no trouble with them though! I just wanna get to our money and get back out of here as fast as we can!'

'I never heard nothing about Apaches being in these parts, Klute!' Craven stammered. 'Ya never told me anything about redskins, Klute! I ain't no Injun fighter!'

Varney stared at the outlaw. In all his days he had never met one as cowardly as Matt Craven. Maybe that was why Craven was such a good killer. Fear of everything which might harm him made Craven's gunhand always find its mark.

'I reckon we better find us another trail back to our hideout, boys!' Varney suggested in a manner that told the three other outlaws that he had already decided on their next actions. 'If we head on the way we're going, them Apache might be able to get the drop on us! There's a hundred narrow trails linking most of these ravines together

112

and a war party of crazed Apaches could spring out on us from anywhere! Nope, we gotta go the long ways round and get to the main canyon from due south!'

'So ya figure it's safer to circle the whole canyon and come in from down yonder, Klute?' Jones asked.

'Yep!'

'But it'll add an hour to our journey!' Craven said.

'It'll also help us keep our scalps!' Kettle nodded with a wry smile. 'I'd kinda like holding on to what little hair I've still got! Looks better on me than it would on a stinking Apache's lance, Matt!'

Craven's face went pale. 'They scalp folks?'

'Yep!' Kettle raised an eyebrow. 'White folks taught them that when they first come to America! Injun scalps made damn pretty wigs for them rich critters back in the old world, I'm told!'

'Stop it, Frog!' Varney said. 'Matt's scared enough as it is without you adding logs to his fire!'

Suddenly the chilling sound of an arrow whistling through the hot air caught their attention. Before any of the four horsemen could locate the archer it drove itself deep into the side of Clu Jones's mount, just behind its shoulder. The animal bucked and threw its master high into the air. Jones landed beneath the hoofs of Kettle's horse. The outlaw scrambled away and looked around the jagged peaks which surrounded them.

'There!' Kettle pointed. Jones' head turned. He saw him.

Jones saw the Apache warrior close to one of the signal fires and the plumes of smoke that billowed upward beside him. The solitary Indian fired another deadly projectile from his small bow.

The arrow sped down at the outlaws. Jones ducked and felt his Stetson being taken from his head.

'That was damn brazen!' Jones ripped the rifle from under Kettle's saddle, cocked its mechanism, raised it to his shoulder and fired one perfect bullet at the high ridge. The Apache buckled, dropped his bow and then toppled forward over the edge of the high rockface.

The four outlaws watched as the Indian's lifeless body fell the several hundred feet. A cloud of dust rose a quarter-mile away from them.

'Damn good shot, Clu!' Varney praised.

Jones tossed the rifle into Kettle's hands and then went to his horse. The animal was down in a kneeling position. Blood pumped from around the arrow in the horse's flesh.

'My horse's finished, Klute!' Jones said angrily.

'Double up with Frog!' Varney ordered. He drew one of his Colts and cocked its hammer.

The others watched as Varney squeezed its trigger and shot the wounded horse straight between

114

its eyes. The animal tumbled on to its side.

'C'mon, Clu!' Kettle pulled his left boot from his stirrup, held out an arm and helped Jones get up behind him. 'Where's there's one Apache, there gotta be more!'

The three mounts and their four burdens swung around.

'C'mon, boys!' Klute Varney spurred his mount. He led them the long way around the rugged canyon. He wanted to make sure he put enough distance between them and the Apaches. He could ill afford to lose a man or another horse in this hostile place. As they rode they watched the jagged peaks above them for any sign of more Indians.

The sound of the two shots still echoed around the high-walled ravines. Iron Eyes swung his horse full circle and listened. He knew the difference between a rifle shot and a pistol shot. He had heard one of each and then silence. It was coming from the direction in which he had seen the outlaws riding when he had been at the very top of the high mountain ridge.

Iron Eyes wondered why the shots had been fired. But he knew that this land had many animals capable of killing full-grown men. As the echo finally faded he turned his attention to his horse.

The bounty hunter looked down at his exhausted mount and knew that unlike himself, it needed water. Iron Eyes could survive on whiskey and cigar smoke but horses were always a problem. Without feed or water they tended to die.

He lifted his canteen and shook it. It was empty. 'Damn it all!' he grumbled, and returned it to his saddle horn. He knew that the animal would never survive to get him out of this baking-hot hell unless he watered it. And watered it soon.

Iron Eyes ran the palm of his right hand over his throbbing left arm. It made him grit his teeth. He snorted hard and found a twisted half-used cigar in his coat pocket. He struck a match with his thumb-nail and inhaled.

Although it angered him, Iron Eyes knew that he had to take a short detour and ride to the closest waterhole.

To his knowledge, there were just two small waterholes within riding distance. Both were at least thirty minutes away from the mouth of the main canyon. Either would take him in the wrong direction.

Iron Eyes blew a line of smoke at the ground and turned the animal's head. He spurred and rode towards the waterhole he considered to be the closest.

By the time Iron Eyes reached the small water-hole his mount was almost spent. It now could no longer find any pace faster than walking. For the first time since he had bought the horse the

116

animal was unresponsive to the spurs that he continued to stab into its sweat-covered body. Exhaustion had now overwhelmed its fear of the man on its saddle.

The bounty hunter dismounted slowly. He gave a long sigh and released the reins. The horse left him, walked to the waterhole and dropped its head towards the water.

By the time Iron Eyes had caught up with it the animal had almost drunk its fill. With his bony hands the bounty hunter opened the saddle-bag satchel and pulled out his whiskey bottle. He sat down on the sand and watched his mount continue to drink as he uncorked the bottle and lifted it to his dry lips. He had taken only two swallows when he was abruptly halted by the sound his mount made.

It was a sickening noise.

It was the sound a horse can make only when in agony.

Iron Eyes lowered the bottle and watched as the horse staggered backwards. It was shaking, then white foam came from its mouth.

The tall man got back to his feet. He stared in disbelief as the animal made even more pitiful noises before crashing on to the sand.

Iron Eyes had never liked horses but knew that without them he would never have been able to chase all the men who had bounty on their heads.

117

Slowly he walked to the animal and watched as more foam poured from its open mouth. A chill swept over him. He took another swig of whiskey and then glanced at the innocent-looking water-hole.

He leaned over and scooped some of the water up in the palm of his hand. He raised it to his nose and sniffed it.

'Poison!' Iron Eyes said. He shook the water away, lifted the bottle and took another mouthful of the whiskey. He swallowed and then glanced briefly at the dying horse. 'Ya should have copied me, horse! Don't see me drinking water!'

Iron Eyes knew he had to put the animal out of its misery. He went to pull one of his guns free when he recalled how close the outlaws and Buffalo Benson were. He did not want to advertise the fact that they had unexpected company in the canyon.

The bounty hunter pushed the cork back into the neck of the bottle and slid it into his coat pocket. He leaned down and wrapped his fingers around the hilt of the Bowie knife. He withdrew it from the boot neck and gave a shake of his head.

He stepped over the neck of the horse, ignoring the pain in his left arm, and grabbed at the animal's mane. He jerked the head back and quickly ran the sharp blade across the horse's throat.

118

As he wiped the blood off the blade on his pants leg he gave a fleeting glance upward at the jagged rocks. For a brief second he saw something up there.

His nostrils flared. He could track the scent of anything as long as he was downwind. His hunting instincts had never let him down and they told his every fibre what was up on the top of the high ridge.

'Apache!' Iron Eyes said. 'And where's there's an Apache there has to be a pony! And I need me a pony!'

Iron Eyes pushed the knife back into his boot and started to climb. Even pain and fever could not stop the hunter of men when he had the scent of his prey in his nostrils.

Buffalo Benson had positioned himself, his mount and the packhorse carrying the body of Duke Layne well towards the end of the long, wide ravine. Apart from a narrow crack in the rocks which was little wider than a horse, it came to a dead end. He had found a fallen boulder so big it was capable of concealing him from the eyes of anyone who entered the ravine. He, like Iron Eyes, had spotted the four outlaws heading on the same route as he had taken. Benson knew it was far easier for him to let the outlaws show him where their hideout was than try and locate it himself.

119

Once he knew that secret he could strike and get his hands on the reputed fortune Klute Varney had stashed.

If the stories he had heard were correct, it would add up to a far greater sum than the bounty on their heads.

Like a massive bear Benson crouched behind the huge boulder and watched along the length of the ravine for signs of the riders' approach. He had no watch to tell him how long he had waited but he was thinking it had been far longer than he had expected. He too had heard the distant shots and wondered what had happened to the riders.

Perhaps the men he had spotted had not been the outlaws but four other riders.

Then unexpectedly his attention was drawn to something on the other side of the canyon. The sun had crept to the opposite rockface and was reflecting off something. The huge bounty hunter straightened up and lowered his rifle. Only something metal glinted when the rays of the sun flashed across it, he told himself.

There should be no metal on a solid wall of rock. Something was glinting, though, and beckoning him to investigate further.

Although it was heavily camouflaged Benson suddenly knew that his quest for the outlaws' hideout was over. It was there staring him right in the face.

Without even thinking he dropped his Winchester and ran towards it. His powerful hands tore the rocks away to reveal a crude wooden door braced against a cave entrance. A metal handle gleamed as sunlight danced across it.

'Got ya!' Benson laughed out loud and ripped the door away in one effortless movement. It crashed at his side and he looked into the dark cave mouth.

His eyes widened. He had found it.

Benson stepped inside. His eyes adjusted quickly to the dim light. He saw the three boxes stacked against the cave wall and rushed to them. His strong fingers tore at the lids and found cans of food in the first one. He tossed the box aside.

The second was full to overflowing with cash. The huge man could not believe his eyes as he focused on the thousands of bank notes. There was no bill lower than fifty dollars in denomination. After stuffing his clothing with as many of the banknotes as he could manage he saw the third box. This one had its lid nailed down firmly.

Benson was not easily deterred from his task. He pulled one of his guns from its holster and started to smash the wooden lid until it caved in.

The bounty hunter's mouth fell open.

He gasped and began to shake as he saw the gleaming gold bars catch the light from the cave entrance.

121

'Gold!' Benson stammered. 'There must be twenty bars of gold in here! I'm rich! I'm richer than a king!'

Using his incredible strength, Benson lifted the box off the ground and staggered out into the daylight. He laboured over every step until he reached the two horses. After dropping the box on to the sand Benson pulled a knife from his belt and cut at the rope which was holding the rotting body of Duke Layne on the packhorse. He pulled the body off the animal and kicked it away. Then he hoisted the box up on to the back of the horse. He secured it firmly.

'Ha!' He laughed. 'This must be worth a million bounties!'

Benson rubbed his hands together and raced back to the cave to get the paper money. He lifted the box full of cash and walked back out into the bright sunlight. He could not imagine the value of his discovery but knew that it had to be thousands. Maybe even tens of thousands.

With each step the sum grew in his fertile mind. 'I could be one of them millionaires I read about! I could be the richest varmint in Utah!'

The bounty hunter suddenly felt something brush at his hairy neck. At first he thought it had been a fly. Then the sound of a rifle firing echoed all around him.

Benson rolled over and blinked in disbelief. He

raised a hand and felt the blood on his neck. He stared at it as another bullet ripped into the box beside him. Bank notes flew up into the air and then fell like snow all around him.

The huge man tore his bandanna from his neck and stuffed it against the grazed flesh. The blood was still pumping but he had no time to fret.

He crawled across the sand as bullets ripped up the canyon floor all around him. Eventually he managed to reach the relative safety of the boulder. He pressed his back against it as more bullets tore at the rocks.

Choking dust exploded all over him. Benson was confused and more than a little worried. He tore a leather strip from his fringed jacket and tied it around his neck until it was almost choking him.

The blood-flow slowed.

He groped for his guns and found them. He drew them from their holsters and turned to where the firing was coming from. He fired both weapons in quick succession until half their bullets had sped to where the rifle shots were coming from.

For a moment there was no response.

Then it came.

At least fifty rounds were returned with venom.

The side of the boulder was riddled as chunks of stone came flying off and showered over the bounty hunter.

123

'Who are they?' Benson asked himself. 'Is this Varney and his scum?'

It would not be long before he discovered the answer.

THIRTEEN

The sound of gunplay echoed all around Devil's Canyon. It would not cease its chilling fusillade. There was a battle going on somewhere but Iron Eyes could only guess at who was fighting and why. But none of that mattered to the wounded man. He had another more urgent priority. He had to get a horse as quickly as he could to give himself a chance of ever escaping this unholy place when he had achieved his goal.

Somehow Iron Eyes had managed to ignore totally the constant pain in his left arm,. He climbed the rockface in less than ten minutes. A few feet from the lip of the ridge he paused and cautiously raised his head so that he could see whether his instincts had been proved right.

They had been.

His eyes narrowed as they spied the Apache warrior kneeling next to a pile of bone-dry kindling on the flat plateau.

Iron Eyes' long bony fingers reached up, caught hold of the sharp rocks and pulled his lean body up over the edge. He lay flat for a few seconds, watching as the Indian struck one small rock against another trying to create a spark that would ignite the kindling and create a fire. His attention shifted to the young pony.

That would do just fine, he thought.

The bounty hunter knew he was downwind of the Indian. He could smell the unmistakable scent of the Apache but knew his own deathly aroma would not reach the Indian's nostrils. Not unless the wind changed dramatically.

The blanket which lay beside the kneeling man was going to be used to make smoke signals, Iron Eyes concluded. It had come from the back of the small brown-and-white pony, which stood a mere twenty feet away close to the steep trail up which the Apache had ridden to reach this high vantage point.

Iron Eyes slipped quietly out of his long coat and pulled the Bowie knife from his boot. He then started to crawl towards his target.

His well-honed hunting skills were now guiding Iron Eyes. Now he knew that he did not have to think of what to do next. Now he would simply act and react. It was hunter against prey, as it had always been.

126

The kneeling Apache was oblivious to the danger that was creeping up on his blind side. By the time he glanced back, it was already too late.

The horrific sight of Iron Eyes with the knife gripped between his teeth was enough to startle even the most heroic of souls. Few had survived more than a few seconds when faced by this apparition. The Apache tried to turn on his knees. He threw both rocks at the bounty hunter. They hit Iron Eyes right in the head, but that did not stop the determined man's advance.

The brave drew his own knife.

Both men rose like rutting stags. They engaged. They locked in battle with hands and knives taking the place of antlers.

The knives flashed in the blazing sunlight as both fighters lashed out. Iron Eyes gripped the Indian's wrist and then felt his own knife hand encircled by strong, unyielding fingers.

The smaller, stronger Indian managed to force Iron Eyes back towards the very edge of the precipice. Iron Eyes tried to dig his boots in and prevent his light frame from being pushed off the edge. The Apache knew that he had the advantage. He was closer to the ground and so able to muster far more strength than his wounded opponent.

The bounty hunter felt his left boot slip. He drew his head back and then brought it down on the face of the painted warrior. The violence of the head butt dazed them both. The Apache released his grip and staggered backwards.

That was all Iron Eyes needed. A mere split second to gain the advantage over the stronger man. He fell on to his knees, then turned the knife in his hand so that its blade was now aimed upwards. The stunned Apache shook his head and came back at him with ferocious speed.

Iron Eyes dropped a shoulder, stretched out his arm and watched as the blade of his knife sank deeply into the belly of his charging foe.

The Indian stopped in full flight. All expression disappeared from his face. He fell on to his side next to the panting bounty hunter. Iron Eyes dragged the knife free and then got back to his feet. He spat at the Apache, plucked his coat off the ground and made as though to walk away.

The dying Apache shouted at him.

With no sign of mercy or respect the bounty hunter paused just long enough to look at his defeated enemy. He walked back to the prostrate figure and kicked out with his right boot.

The Indian rolled, then fell over the edge of the high rocks. Iron Eyes leaned out and watched as the body hit the canyon floor. Dust rose from its impact.

'I hate Apaches!' Iron Eyes turned and walked towards the pony. 'I really hate Apaches!'

FOURTEEN

The Indian pony thundered down the steep mountain trail yet no matter how fast it ran it could not escape its new master's bloodied spurs. Iron Eyes showed it no mercy. He wanted to reach the floor of Devil's Canyon and get to grips with the four outlaws who were somewhere within its confines. He knew that their collected bounties would keep him in whiskey and cigars for at least a year.

As Iron Eyes spurred he could still hear the gunfire echoing all around him. He wondered what was going on. Then he recalled seeing his worst enemy, Buffalo Benson, leading a packhorse with a body lashed across its back.

Had Benson decided to try and capture Iron Eyes' chosen prey and collect the reward money on their heads?

It was a thought which drove the bounty hunter

into making his pony find even more pace.

The terrified animal charged down the last yards of the sloping trail and on to the flat sand. Iron Eyes hauled back on the crude rope reins and stopped it in its tracks. His long legs hung almost to the ground as he sat astride the bareback animal. The sound of the shooting carried on. Iron Eyes swung the small pony around in an attempt to locate where it was coming from. It was impossible. The high-sided walls of solid rock were unfamiliar to him. The trail from the high mountain had led him away from the main canyon. Now he was somewhere that he did not recognize.

He gritted his teeth.

'Where the hell am I?' he shouted to himself.

There were three trails away from where his mount was standing. Three choices. Two were wide whilst the third was little more than a crack in the canyon wall. Little wider than the pony he sat upon.

Iron Eyes forced the pony to walk in a wide circle. He listened hard as he passed each of the canyon trails. There had to be a clue to which was the one he should take. The one that would lead him to the fighting and the men he sought.

Which one would get him to the outlaws he craved to meet and destroy?

To his surprise it seemed that the sound of

shooting was coming from the narrowest of the three trails.

Iron Eyes hauled the head of the pony around and stared at the break in the canyon wall which faced him. It looked as though a mythical giant had brought his axe down on the wall of rock and split it.

He edged the pony closer, tilted his head and listened even harder. He was right. This was where the sound of shooting seemed to be loudest. Iron Eyes straightened up. He tried to see down along the length of the trail but it twisted and turned too much. Sunlight could not penetrate into the ravine either. The emaciated man rubbed his arm and realized that it no longer hurt. He flexed his fingers and nodded to himself.

Iron Eyes raised a hand and slapped the rump of the pony as hard as he could. With no saddle or stirrups he had to use every facet of his riding skills just to stay on the pony's back as it bolted into action.

'C'mon, nag!' Iron Eyes yelled. 'I got me some vermin to kill!'

The Indian pony galloped into the twisting crack in the sand-coloured rockface. It would not be allowed to ease its pace until its new master decided it was time to do so.

Klute Varney had been the first to spot the

unknown intruder hauling away their ill-gotten gains. He was also the first to open fire. Within seconds his cohorts had joined him in the relentless show of firepower. They had left their three remaining horses at the mouth of the main canyon and steadily made their way deeper into its fiery heart.

There was plenty of cover. Craven and Varney used every protruding boulder along the rockface for cover as they slowly made their way towards their hideout. Jones and Kettle used the opposite wall in the same manner.

Their rifles were smoking hot as the four men shot their way ever closer to their unknown adversary.

Whoever he was, they had him pinned down.

For more than two long minutes there had been no return fire from the man behind the large boulder.

Varney halted their steady progress with a raised arm. He looked to Craven behind him. Sweat hung on the outlaw who, Varney feared, would one day make a mistake that could cost them all dear. He glanced across at Kettle and Jones. They were on the same side of the canyon as their quarry. The huge boulder behind which the unknown intruder was hiding gave them total protection from his guns.

Varney waved his Colt at his two most reliable

men by way of giving instructions. They understood his silent signals and waved their rifles in
reply.

Craven moved to the shoulder of his leader.

'What ya telling them, Klute?' Craven asked
nervously.

'I'm telling them not to waste ammo, Matt!'
Varney retorted gruffly. 'I'm also telling them to
creep up on that boulder as quiet as they can!'

Craven rubbed the sweat from his face. 'What
about us? What we gonna do?'

Varney turned and looked at the face which was
only inches from his own. He gave it a cruel smile.

'You and me are gonna draw that bastard's fire
and give Frog and Clu a chance of creeping up on
him!'

Craven felt his heart quicken its pace. 'I ain't
drawing fire for nobody! Why should I be a damn
target? Nope! I ain't gonna do it, Klute!'

Varney jerked his .45 around and poked its
barrel up under Craven's chin. He smiled even
wider.

'Oh yes, you are, Matt! If'n ya don't, I'll kill ya
myself!'

Craven gulped hard. 'You serious? You'd kill
me?'

'Yep! I sure would!' Varney grabbed the outlaw's
collar and swung him around. He shook Craven
and stared straight into his eyes. 'Now, me and you

are gonna rush that *hombre* and give the boys a chance to creep up on him! Savvy?'

Matt Craven said nothing.

Suddenly Varney felt the barrel of Craven's own Colt poking him in the guts. Before he could look down his entire body shook as the deafening sound of the gun filled his ears. A pain ripped through his guts. It was unlike anything he had ever experienced before. He teetered backwards for a second and then tried to aim his own pistol.

'You stinking coward!' Varney spat as blood ran from his mouth.

Craven sneered and then fired again. This time he saw the gore splatter from the second brutal wound. Varney twisted in the air and crashed on to the sand.

'What ya doing, Matt?' Kettle shouted out in horror.

'Ya killed Klute!' Jones yelled in disbelief.

Craven raised his gun and aimed in their direction. 'You wanna make a fight of this, old-timers?'

They sure did.

The two outlaws dropped on to their bellies and started to fire their guns at the younger man. He in turn dropped down behind the crumpled body of Varney and propped it up to act as a shield.

The canyon now echoed with even more gunfire.

Within a few minutes all three had spent their shells and needed to reload. There was a lull as if time itself had stood still whilst the gunfighters shook hot brass casings from their guns and dragged fresh bullets from their belts to replace them.

The battle restarted.

Gunsmoke filled the wide canyon and mixed with the hot air to make a sickening cocktail. Craven blasted his handguns in quick succession. Then Clu Jones screamed and tried to rise to his feet as he realized he had been hit.

'Git down, Clu!' Kettle implored.

It was too late. Even the crazed Craven could not miss a standing target at such distance. Jones was knocked off his feet and tumbled into the canyon wall behind them.

'Give up!' Craven demanded.

Kettle had used up all the rounds in his rifle. He tossed it aside, pulled his .45s and blasted both at once. He saw his bullets tear into the lifeless Varney. He knew that it would take something special to kill the cowardly man who hid behind the corpse.

Then he realized that he did have something special.

Something hidden in his deep jacket pocket.

Something he been keeping secret from his fellow outlaws for over a year. It was something he knew would bring this fight to a sudden and brutal conclusion.

He carefully dug deep and pulled out the dynamite stick from his inside pocket. He blew the dust off it. A smile crossed his weathered features. Then he searched for the short minute fuse he had in his pants pocket.

'Ya run out of ammo, Frog?' Craven yelled out through the gunsmoke that separated them. 'I ain't! I still got me plenty of bullets and I ain't even started to use old Klute's guns yet!'

'Why don't ya come over here and find out, Matt?' Kettle called back as his large fingers pushed the fuse into the soft end of the explosives. 'I'd ask if you was scared but I already know the answer to that 'un! I can smell ya fear from over here, boy!'

'You calling me yella?' Not willing to waste time loading his own guns again, Craven picked up Varney's Colts and cocked their hammers. 'Well? Are ya?'

Kettle pulled a match from his shirt pocket and dragged it up the side of his pants leg. It ignited and he hastily lit the fuse. It burst into spitting fury.

The outlaw licked his dry lips and watched as the fuse burned down quickly. Sixty seconds was not a very long time and the big man knew it. He inhaled and then hoisted the single stick of grade A dynamite across the distance between them. He saw it hit the rocks behind Craven and fall. Kettle buried his face in the hot sand and pushed his fingers in his ears.

The explosion was far bigger than Kettle had thought it would be. The ancient rocks had never been subject to anything as powerful before.

The entire canyon shook.

Boulders started to fall from all sides. Choking dust enveloped the entire floor of the canyon making it impossible for the outlaw to see if he had succeeded in destroying Matt Craven or not.

There was no time to find out.

Faster than a man of his age should have been able to move, Frog Kettle got back to his feet and looked all around him. He was scared. He had not expected the dry canyon walls to fall the way they were falling.

He looked back through the thick swirling dust to where their three horses were. Rocks of every size were falling like shrapnel between the outlaw and the mounts.

Kettle grabbed his rifle and started to make for them as fast as his legs could carry him. It was not easy. He had to avoid the falling debris as best he could.

He had not gone far when he froze in his tracks.

Frog Kettle's eyes widened and his jaw dropped.

Through the dust he could see them.

A line of Apache horsemen were moving

steadily into the mouth of the wide canyon. They were painted for war.

Herinaco and his warriors had arrived.

FIFTEEN

The blood-chilling sound of charging Apaches would have frozen Hell itself with fear. Frog Kettle had never run so fast in all his days. The beefy man raced back up the box canyon as he heard the unshod hoofs behind him start to gather pace. Herinaco and his trusty followers thought that they had found the man who had killed their young braves. They yelled as they urged their ponies on. They did not want to kill this man swiftly. They wanted him to suffer and die a thousand times. They had followed Buffalo Benson's trail to this place and it was Kettle's misfortune that he was the first white man they had encountered in Devil's Canyon.

The outlaw knew that within seconds they would be upon him and that single thought made his legs respond as they had never done before.

The terrified man ran towards the billowing

139

smoke and dust which still hung on the dry air halfway along the canyon. Kettle knew it would give him a chance of escaping the Apaches who seemed intent on capturing him.

The burly man charged into the choking dust. Within a few steps he felt himself falling. The hole that the dynamite had created was huge. The outlaw fell head over heels and crashed beside the remnants of what had once been Craven and Varney.

Finding himself face down between smouldering body parts gave the outlaw a reason to scramble back to his feet quickly. He picked up his rifle and pushed its handguard down. To his horror it was empty. Then he remembered that he had not reloaded it. He tossed it aside.

With every second he could hear the sound of the Apaches getting closer. He climbed out of the crater and crawled to the closest of the fallen rocks. He drew his guns and pulled back their hammers.

The smoke was a curse and also a blessing.

If he had been able to see the Apaches he might have given up there and then. He started to fire his weapons through the dense cloud. Then he raced further up the canyon.

Suddenly bullets came back at Kettle.

They danced off the rocks all around him and forced the outlaw to run even faster away from his unseen enemies.

The Apache war cries were now so loud that the outlaw realized that he had only one option left open to him. He had to stop and try to kill them before they appeared like deadly phantoms through the dust and smoke and turned their venom upon him.

Kettle dropped to his knees as more rifle bullets hit the rockface, causing debris to shower over him. He hastily reloaded both his Colts and started to fire blindly at the noises behind him.

At that very same moment Iron Eyes thundered in from the narrow trail and appeared at the top of the canyon. He pulled the pony to a halt violently using both the rope rein and the animal's flowing mane. The animal fell on to the sand heavily and its new master cartwheeled across the ground like a rag doll.

Iron Eyes gritted his teeth. He rose with both his Navy Colts in his bony hands. His eyes darted all around as they tried vainly to see who was shooting at whom.

Then he saw the figure to his left crouching behind a huge boulder beside two nervous horses. It did not take more than the blink of an eye for Iron Eyes to recognize his deadly rival.

As Iron Eyes got back to his feet he shouted the name as though it, like its owner, was poison.

'Benson!'

Buffalo Benson had been keeping himself hidden for more than five minutes. First it had been the outlaws, who for some reason had turned upon each other and forgotten about him. Then he had heard the unmistakable sound of the Apaches. In all that time he remained behind the rock which gave him protection from the eyes and bullets of those who would otherwise certainly try to kill him.

Now he was looking straight at the man who he knew would never do a deal to let him go. Iron Eyes never made deals with those he despised. And he despised Benson more than any of the prey he hunted so ruthlessly.

'Iron Eyes!' Benson growled in a low tone designed to be heard only by the bounty hunter.

Iron Eyes' attention darted between the large man and the commotion a hundred yards down the canyon. A ruckus concealed by the dust and smoke.

The Navy Colts were held at hip level. They were trained on Benson as his long thin legs drew Iron Eyes closer to the huge boulder and the back-shooting man it concealed from those who were fighting.

'What ya skulking there for?' Iron Eyes snapped the question like a rattler attacking its victim. 'And what's going on down there?'

'I dunno, Iron Eyes!' Benson answered. His

fingers curled around the Winchester in his hands. 'I'm just an innocent critter caught up in this!'

Iron Eyes stopped walking. 'You damn liar! Them Apaches are after somebody who done something bad! I reckon it's a safe bet that you're the one they really want!'

'Right again, Iron Eyes!' A crooked smile carved its way across Benson's face. He took a deep breath and squared up to the tall, thin figure standing less than twenty feet from him. His hands were sweating. The fingers of his right hand crept into the guard of the repeating rifle. 'I figure them Apaches are kinda upset by my killing a few of their young 'uns!'

'A few?'

Benson's smile grew. 'OK! Maybe seven or eight of their young bucks! Who cares? They're just stinking Apaches!'

Iron Eyes stared at the man. He could hear the fight getting more ferocious further along the canyon. Bullets were still being fired by guns and rifles.

'I don't like Apaches myself but that's cos they don't like me none! But I got me another question!'

'What question?' Benson snapped. He knew he had the Winchester ready for action and it would only take a fraction of a second for him to raise it and fire.

143

'How'd ya get out of jail so fast?' Iron Eyes asked. 'Sheriff Bodine had ya locked up nice and tight!'

Benson gave a chuckle. 'Snake bust me out!'

'Snake Peters?'

Benson nodded. 'Yep!'

'Where is he now?'

'Knockin' on Heaven's door!'

'Reckon the Devil don't know he's dead yet then!' Iron Eyes said. Once again his eyes flashed to the sound of the still unseen commotion.

'Maybe not!'

'How'd Snake bust you out of jail exactly?' Iron Eyes knew that Benson must have already cranked the rifle's mechanism. He also knew that it was only a matter of time before it was turned on him. The only thing preventing that deadly manoeuvre was the fact that any shot fired now might bring the Apaches on them. So far the Indians did not seem to realize that either of the bounty hunters was there behind the large smooth boulder. 'Snake pay your bail?'

'Nope!' Benson grinned.

Iron Eyes took another step forward. 'Then how?'

'He kinda killed that old sheriff for me!'

'On your orders?'

'Sure!' Benson replied. 'Snake never done nothing without my telling him first!'

'You're even lower than I thought ya were, Buffalo!' Iron Eyes said. 'Killing a lawman just cos he got ya locked up? Why do that?'

Benson hands were shaking. He wanted to end this now but knew that for either of them to open up with their weaponry would alert the Apaches. He did not want to die a rich man without a scalp.

'Answer me!' Iron Eyes shouted.

'Keep ya damn voice down, Iron Eyes!' Benson urged. 'You'll bring them redskins down on us!'

'I ain't scared of Apaches, Buffalo!' Iron Eyes took another step. His guns were still levelled at the larger man.

Suddenly the shooting stopped. Both men turned and looked to where the cloud of dust and smoke hung. They could hear the unshod ponies galloping away. The triumphant whoops of those who thought that they had achieved their goal echoed off the canyon walls.

Both Benson and Iron Eyes knew that someone had paid the ultimate price of being mistaken for the man the Apaches actually sought.

After a few seconds the noise of the hoofbeats faded.

Herinaco had gone.

Slowly the two bounty hunters returned their attention to one another again. Now both men knew that there was nothing to fear.

Nothing except the guns and rifle in each

other's hands.

'Ya got lucky!' Iron Eyes stated. 'Them Apaches think they killed ya!'

'Yep!' Benson chuckled. 'Cryin' shame!'

'What ya doing here? You after the bounty on these outlaws' heads like me?' Iron Eyes asked.

Benson suddenly realized that his deadly foe had not noticed the fortune tied to the back of his packhorse. He gritted his teeth and stepped away from the boulder.

'Yep! That's it! The bounty!'

'My bounty!' Iron Eyes corrected.

'OK!' Benson shrugged as his hands nursed the rifle. 'You can have it! Keep the bounty!'

Iron Eyes did not know much about Buffalo Benson but one thing he did know was that Benson never gave up that easy. He'd skin his own mother for a few bucks. Something was not quite right. His head tilted. His eyes burned into the big man.

'Ya giving me the bounty?'

'Yep!'

Iron Eyes almost smiled. 'OK! Reckon ya must have turned over a new leaf!'

'Why don't ya lower them hoglegs, then?'

The tall thin figure did lower his lethal hand-guns. But they were still cocked and his fingers still curled around their triggers. He shrugged and turned away.

146

'Much obliged, Buffalo!'

Benson could not resist the temptation. Iron Eyes was walking away, intending to find what was left of the four outlaws' bodies. Benson swung around, raised the Winchester and fired quickly.

The bullet went straight through the tails of Iron Eyes' long trail coat. It did not hit the thin man inside its bloodstained fabric though.

Iron Eyes twisted, raised his Colts and fired both .38s in quick succession.

Buffalo Benson felt the two bullets hit him. They jolted him back with the power of a mule kick. He went to push the handguard down again to bring another bullet into the rifle's magazine when two more shots punched him off his feet.

Iron Eyes, like the guns in his hands, smouldered. He stared at the body and then spat on it.

'Ya know something, Buffalo?' Iron Eyes asked the corpse before he headed on down the canyon in search of the outlaws' bodies. 'I hated you even more than I hates Apaches! Unlike them, though, I figure I've seen the last of you!'

In less than an hour Iron Eyes had rustled up the three outlaw horses and secured the remains of Duke Layne and Frog Kettle on to one of them and that of Clu Jones to another. The third horse he would use himself. It had angered him that the other two outlaws had been blown into so many bits that it was impossible to recognize them. To claim bounty money on outlaws' heads you needed the heads and Iron Eyes had not been able to find either Varney's or Craven's anywhere.

Apart from plucking the rotting body of Duke Layne off the sand next to that of Buffalo Benson's, Iron Eyes had not paid any attention to the horse laden down with the hefty box of gold bars. The exhausted Iron Eyes had not paid any heed to the box filled with cash either.

Having no knowledge of the outlaws' hideout or what had been secreted within it, Iron Eyes had only concentrated upon the bounties.

Before leaving Devil's Canyon he rode to the poisoned waterhole and found his dead mount. He retrieved his rifle, but in truth it was only the weathered saddle-bags and their contents that he actually wanted.

Iron Eyes drank what was left of the whiskey and started a new cigar.

A trail of smoke floated over his shoulder as he drove on at brutal speed. He was thirsty and knew he would have to return to Silver Springs to quench that thirst.

There were many ways out of this maze of ravines but he would take the same route out of Devil's Canyon as the one which had brought him to this devilish place. Iron Eyes spurred his new horse up the steep trail and led the pair of animals burdened with the dead outlaws' bodies behind him.

There was now an increased sense of urgency in the bounty hunter and it was nothing to do with his craving for hard liquor.

He had shaken off the fever and the incredible pain from his wound but knew that somewhere around the blistering sand-coloured rocks there were deadly Apaches.

Apaches who had tasted blood this day and might wish to savour its flavour again should they encounter him in their heartland. For the bounty hunter knew that he was a prize all Apaches wanted.

The Apaches had yet to discover the warrior he had killed in order to steal his pony. Once they did Iron Eyes knew it would be suicidal for him to remain here.

Iron Eyes gazed at the sky as he rode ever upwards.

It had turned red as the sun slowly began to set.

He spurred hard and thought about the sand far below him. A sand which had been even redder with the blood of men.

Darkness could not come fast enough for the bounty hunter.

FINALE

A thousand lights illuminated the small border town of Silver Springs as the lone rider approached it from the south. It stood like a jewelled necklace in the darkness. Iron Eyes could not recall when he had last rested or slept. One day had melted into another until all he knew for sure was that he had achieved most of what he had set out to do. He had managed to bring the bodies of three outlaws back. One of them was partly responsible for the gruesome slayings in the hotel. His partner in crime was now a meal for the vultures and animals of Devil's Canyon.

Iron Eyes steered the lathered-up horse beneath him slowly down the main street with the two others in tow. He rode past the sheriff's office and continued on towards the building where he knew he would find Doc Jackson.

If anyone knew who was in charge of Silver

Springs law now that Bodine was dead, it would be the elderly medicine man.

People stopped in the streets outside the stores and saloons which remained open. They watched silently as the emaciated bounty hunter rode quietly along the dusty street. Few had ever seen a man looking almost as dead as the bodies he had in his possession.

The amber lantern-light which flooded from all directions bathed Iron Eyes in a softer hue. Yet even this could not hide the horrific scars he bore from the onlookers' gaze.

None of those who watched dared come close to Iron Eyes as he drew up to the hitching pole directly below the doctor's second-floor office.

The bounty hunter threw his long right leg over the neck of the tired horse and slid to the ground. He tied the reins firmly to the rail and then ensured that the pack-animals were also unable to escape with their valuable cargoes.

'Iron Eyes!'

The voice was familiar. Iron Eyes turned and looked at the man who was walking quickly down the sheltered boardwalk toward him. It was Doc Jackson.

'Doc!' Iron Eyes acknowledged.

The doctor stopped and looked at the bodies tied across the backs of the horses. He felt his mouth dry.

151

'You kill them, boy?'

Iron Eyes moved under the streetlight. 'Nope! I just swept the varmints up and brung them here to collect the reward money!'

Jackson sighed.

'Are any of these the men who shot up the hotel and wounded little Holly?'

Iron Eyes nodded. 'One of them is! The other got himself blown apart by somebody! I ain't figured out who killed who yet! But they're all dead! That's what counts!'

Jackson noticed the fresh bloodstain on the torn sleeve of his trail coat. He went to touch it when the cold eyes stopped him.

'Ya wounded, boy! Let me look at it!'

'Don't fret none! It's OK now, Doc!' Iron Eyes muttered. 'My whiskey tended it just fine!'

The door of the doctor's office opened and Andrew Barker looked down at the two men talking at the foot of the wooden steps. The wealthy businessman saw the bodies and walked down towards them.

'Are you Iron Eyes?' Barker asked. 'My name's Andrew Barker!'

'Yep! Who might you be exactly, Mr Barker?' Iron Eyes stared at the strangely clean man before him.

'I'm the father of little Holly, Iron Eyes!' Barker said holding out his hand. 'I wish to shake your hand in gratitude for what you did! Thank you! Thank you!'

Iron Eyes shook the hand and then turned to look at the three bodies on the horses.

'Either of you know who I can get the bounty money from for bringing in these three killers?'

Jackson rubbed his chin. 'I'm not sure. The sheriff was killed by those bounty hunters, y'know?'

'Buffalo Benson was one of them, Iron Eyes!' Barker added.

'I know!' Iron Eyes returned his icy stare to Barker. 'I evened up that score! I left his carcass back at Devil's Canyon for the vultures!'

'You killed him?' Barker gasped.

'Yep!'

'Why didn't you bring him back with you?' Barker asked. 'I put up a thousand dollars' reward money for his hide when he killed Sheriff Bodine, Iron Eyes!'

The bounty hunter looked hard at both men. 'A thousand bucks reward? For Benson?'

'Yes!' Barker affirmed.

Iron Eyes moved to the two packhorses. He untied the three bodies and pushed them on to the sand.

'Could you make sure that I get the reward for these critters, Doc?' Iron Eyes asked.

Barker stepped forward and placed a hand

upon the tall man's wide bony shoulder.

'I'll honour the bounty for these outlaws! Tell me how much it is and I'll pay you right now!'

Iron Eyes tilted his head. '*You*'ll pay me?'

'Indeed!' Barker confirmed. 'I shall get reimbursed by the authorities later!'

Iron Eyes pulled out two crumpled wanted posters and handed them to Barker.

'That's for Craven and Layne!' Iron Eyes said. 'I ain't sure what these other critters are worth! Maybe the sheriff had posters on them in his office!'

Barker opened his wallet and peeled off several bills. He handed them to the bounty hunter.

'We'll find out what you're owed in the morning!'

'Much obliged, Mr Barker!' Iron Eyes pushed the money into his coat pocket. He then stepped in his stirrup and hoisted himself back on to the back of his horse.

Barker held the horse's bridle. 'Where are you going?'

'I'm going back to Devil's Canyon!' Iron Eyes replied.

'What for, boy?' Jackson piped up.

'To get the stinking carcass of Buffalo Benson, Doc!'

Both Barker and Jackson looked in amazement at one another and then returned their attention

154

to the mounted man. It was Barker who spoke first.

'There's no need for you to go and get his body, Iron Eyes!' Barker said. 'I believe you when you say that Benson is dead! I'll pay you the reward money here and now!'

'Listen to him, boy!' Jackson implored. 'Ya too tuckered to go off again tonight! Get some rest!'

'Thank ya kindly!' Iron Eyes accepted the ten hundred-dollar bills and then added them to the rest of the money in his deep pocket.

'Holly's been asking about you, Iron Eyes!' Barker stated.

Iron Eyes looked down. He could not hide his puzzlement from the well-dressed man. 'Why would she be asking about me?'

'Because you're the man who saved her!'

'The doc saved her!' Iron Eyes argued. 'Not me!'

Jackson leaned on the hitching rail. 'I'd not have had anything to save if not for ya quick reactions in bringing her to me, boy! You saved her life!'

'Come up and see her, Iron Eyes!' Barker urged. 'I'll wake her for you!'

Iron Eyes shook his head. His face looked troubled.

'No! She ain't ever gonna see me!'

'Why not?'

Iron Eyes ran his bony fingers through his mane

of black hair and gave a sigh. He looked down at the father of the child he had saved with a hint of envy.

'Your daughter is asleep and having herself sweet girl dreams! Dreams only young 'uns can have! If she laid eyes on me, those dreams would become nightmares, Mr Barker! I ain't gonna be responsible for making that child afraid to close her eyes at night!'

Andrew Barker suddenly knew what the scarred man meant. He held his hand to his mouth and watched as the horseman pulled his reins free and then turned the mount away from them.

'Where are you going, Iron Eyes?'

'I'm going to get me some whiskey, Mr Barker!'

'And then what are ya gonna do?' Jackson asked as the horse was steered out into the middle of the street and aimed towards the nearest saloon.

'And then I'm gonna get me some more whiskey, Doc!' Iron Eyes called out over his shoulder.

'And vittles, boy!' Jackson ordered. 'Please get something to eat!'

'After the whiskey, Doc! After the whiskey!'

Both men watched in awe as Iron Eyes rode slowly through the cascading lantern-light towards the sound of a tinny piano and the aroma of stale sawdust. Barker thought about the words the bounty hunter had uttered. Sad but wise words.

They turned and started to walk back up to the office and the sleeping child who would never set eyes upon the man who saved her.